Eerey Tocsin on the
UNDERWATER ISLAND

Coding by
Kevin Noel Olson

Illustrations by
Debi Hammack

Eerey Tocsin on the Underwater Island
by Kevin Noel Olson

A Cornerstone Book
Published by Cornerstone Book Publishers
Story Copyright © 2008 by Kevin Noel Olson
Illustrations Copyright © 2008 by Debi Hammack

Cornerstone Book Publishers
New Orleans, LA

First Cornerstone Edition - 2008

www.cornerstonepublishers.com

ISBN: 1-934935-17-4
ISBN 13: 978-1-934935-17-0

MADE IN THE USA

Dedication

This book is for Aiden, Dylan, and all those who are to come. You
fill the world with hope.

-K.N.O.

What do you build with sails for flight?
I build a boat for Sorrow,
O, swift on the seas all day and night
Saileth the rover Sorrow,
All day and night.

-W.B. YEATS

Introduction

One thing I discovered while researching the accounts this book is based on is that jellyfish hurt when they sting you. My experiences with that don't matter. It's just an observation. I would strongly recommend avoiding jellyfish. Never, ever, never-even-ever in Neverland get one stuck inside your diving helmet.

Unfortunately, I must report my investigation did not yield results that entirely confirm nor deny the testimony from Eerey's diary. However, I was able to confirm some relevant information and many of the facts relayed in the account.

The underwater city does exist, as confirmed by a Kanutian I found attending a nearby college. He would speak only on the condition that I not reveal his identity in any greater detail than I have already done. He described the city in detail, all in agreement with diary. He allowed me an undersea voyage by submarine to confirm some important points. I remained locked in my room on the submarine to protect the location of the underwater island. The visit was not approved by the Kanutian government, and I only saw the island from a distance. It did appear to have the reed forest, returning quickly from the damage done to it by the nuclear Kraken. Green people swam in the city, as far as I could tell through the periscope. A young kraken swam by, confirming that portion of the diary. I saw an Otterman as well. I pleaded to see the gigantic creature you will learn about near the end of this book, but fear from the pilot allowed only that I see the lights.

As to where the island is, I might offer only a guess. It comes to mind it may be the Sunken Land of Buss. That particular island was reported by sailors for centuries. Unfortunately, the warm climate where I saw the island does not support exactly Buss Island, as it seemed to be off the coast of Iceland according to reports. A friend suggested it may be the lost city of Atlantis or the sunken continent of Mu. Without more specific details it is hard to judge which of the many, many sunken lands it may be. Only one thing is for certain-jellyfish hurt when they sting you. Take it from me, you don't want one in your diving helmet.

Sincerely,
Kevin Noel Olson

Eerey Tocsin
on the Underwater Island

Chapter 1
GIANT TEETH

A strange, antique and unique submarine floated slightly below the ocean's surface. The shape of a gigantic swordfish, with round viewports decorating its riveted sides, the ship glided effortlessly through the water. The words S.S. Aunt Alice ran along its iron surface. A pair of large, bubble windows stared like eyes behind its long metal snout. In the metal fish's belly, Eerey Tocsin sat at a desk. She crouched over dismantled pieces of a laptop computer and what appeared to be some kind of antique typewriter.

Many of you will remember Eridona 'Eerey' Tocsin dressed in her long, white dress of a bygone era from her adventures in the Cryptoid Zoo. Some of you will be pleased to meet this un-usual girl here. A single, five-watt light bulb swung above her head. It dimly illuminated the metal walls. Despite the weak light, she wore stylish-at-some-point-in-the-past sunglasses. Even the scant yellowish wane from the bulb hurt her sensitive eyes. You might wonder where Eerey's parents were. The exact same thought played on her mind as she worked.

Eerey's parents disappeared along with Mr. Cryptic for a test flight of the old cargo plane meant to return them home from the Cryptoid Zoo. Mr. Cryptic went along to offer pointers and directions. The three never returned; with or without a trace. The plane did not return by itself either.

After waiting a good while, Eerey and her hair-covered cousin Edict decided to search for them. They used the flight plan her father left as a guide. They took the Aunt Alice from the dock. Three talking gorillas manned the submarine as crew. They took along Loofah the orangutaur. An orangutaur was and is a half-orangutan and half-horse. They also took Guy Guess, an invisible boy.

The sound of feet running down the hallway ruined Eerey's concentration. She looked up as the large, metal wheel in the center of the metal door twisted. The rusty hinges creaked loudly. The door swung open. It slammed against the wall with a clang. Loofah and Edict rushed in. Loofah's orangutan body and head seemed misplaced on his Shetland pony body and legs. Seawater dripped off him in pools. His horseshoed-hooves clanged against the metal floor.

Edict came in wearing a pair of swim trunks. The hair that covered his body grew back in short tufts after he lost it during their last adventure.

"Don't!" Eerey shouted as Edict and Loofah rushed over to her. "You'll get the computer wet and ruin it!"

"Eerey!" Edict exclaimed as he and Loofah stopped short. "Is that the laptop mom gave you for our birthday? Mom's not going to be happy that you pulled it apart."

Nodding, Eerey picked up a soldering iron and sighed. "Yes, it is the laptop mom gave me for my birthday. I'm not doing anything wrong with it, and I can explain it all when we find them."

"What are you doing to it?" Loofah asked.

Eerey furrowed her brow as she soldered a circuit board to the old typewriter. "Improving it."

Loofah laughed. "Improving it? You're soldering it to a rusty piece of junk typewriter!"

Eerey looked up, her darkish-red hair falling around the olive skin of her cheeks. She imitated Loofah's laugh. "Shows what you know," she snorted. "Typewriter!"

"It's not a typewriter?" Loofah asked. "What is it?"

Eerey walked toward them. "Look. You two just burst in here like there's something important. Is there?"

Edict nodded excitedly, all but forgetting about the typewriter. "Giant teeth!"

Edict pulled a rag off the desk and wiped water off his face. "Have you two been swimming?" Eerey asked.

"Yes," Loofah replied. "That's what we came to tell you!"

"You came to tell me you've been swimming? That's nice."

Edict shook his head. Black ink now covered his face as Eerey used the cloth to clean the typewriter. She stifled a laugh at the purple hue it gave his face. "No, no! We came here to tell you what happened to Guy while we we swam!"

She removed her glasses. "Something's happened to Guy?"

Edict nodded emphatically. "Yes! That's what we've been trying to tell you! We were swimming outside the ship because we're close to the surface and it's dark so we wouldn't burn."

Eerey walked out the door. "If that's what you've been trying to tell me, why is it the first time I've heard of it since you two walked in? Where is he now?"

Loofah and Edict followed her down the hallway. "He'll be okay," Loofah assured. "He's in the infirmary with the talking apes. They are trying to bandage up his wound."

"Wound!?" Eerey walked a little faster. "What wound?"

"He cut his arm on the giant teeth!" Edict shouted as he tried to keep up. Eerey stopped at the open infirmary door. Three gorilla dressed in navy attire gathered around an empty chair and wrapped gauze around the empty air over the chair. One gorilla wore a captain's suit and hat. The other two wore white sailors' uniforms. All of the gorillas wrapped a figure on the hospital bed. The thickly-piled gauze took on the rough shape of a young boy. Eerey looked at the paper-Mache mess wriggling under their attempts.

Eerey waved the gorillas away. "I'll take over from here." The gorillas grunted as they walked out of the room, pushing aside the gaping Edict and Loofah.

Resting her hands on her hips, Eerey looked at Guy Guess, the invisible boy. He was wrapped up haphazardly in gauze. She began to unravel the mess.

"Hello Guy. What happened to you?" Eerey looked into Guy's bright, blue eyes that only she could see. Eerey feared the dark. So much so she spent a great deal of time in darkness to hone her vision. The practice helped her see what lurked in the night. It also helped her see Guy.

Guy smiled at Eerey, quite pleased to see and be seen by a friend. "The talking gorillas meant to take care of me. Since they can't see me they didn't help much."

Eerey tore off a piece of gauze and wrapped it around Guy's invisible arm. "It doesn't look bad, Guy. You're just bleeding a little. I'll get it wrapped up. Edict said something about giant teeth. What on earth is he talking about?"

Guy nodded, but only Eerey saw. "I hope I'm not buzzing too loudly," he shouted. Eerey shook her head.

"Not much more than a quiet hum in this light," she assured. "It's pretty dark inside the ship."

"Good," he said a little quieter. "I think he's talking about the set of giant teeth that came at me, but I don't think it was actually after me. I tried to swim away, and one of the teeth nicked my arm."

4

"What kind of teeth were they, and how 'giant' were they? Were they giant cow's teeth?"

Guy shook his head. "No. They were sharp as razors and like a shark's. There were a bunch of them and they were about the length of my head."

"Were they attached to anything?"

It was Edict's turn to shake his head. "It's dark out there, and all we saw was the sharp teeth floating like a huge set of carnivore dentures. It could have swallowed us whole."

Eerey shrugged. "Could it have been a gigantic black shark you couldn't see because it was too dark?"

Loofah pulled at the hair on his orangutaur chin. "It's possible."

Sounds like you would have been lucky to have been swallowed whole. Teeth like that could tear you apart! They must have been like razors. The cut on Guy's arm is straight." She stood back to examine the bandages. "I've stopped the bleeding, Guy. You'll be okay as long as it doesn't get infected."

Eerey sighed. "You shouldn't have been swimming in the dark. If it was a black Megalodon shark, that's extremely dangerous. They can be a hundred feet long. That's a third of a football field!"

Edict sneezed as he pulled a navy jacket off a hook on the wall and put it on. "We're way smaller than that! What would something that big want with us?"

Eerey smiled at the thought of Loofah and Edict wrapped up in candy wrappers. "Bite sized snacks."

"Ewww!" Loofah protested. "You'll give me nightmares!"

"It's just like a Rorschach test," Eerey shrugged. "I just say the first thing that comes to mind."

An alarm bell began to ring. "What's that?" Edict asked as he ran into the hall. Loofah and Eerey rushed after him as he ran to the control room. They entered the room to find the talking gorillas looking out the bubble windows. A set of enormous teeth headed for the submarine. A pen attached to a mechanical arm sketched a picture on a stack of paper strapped to a table with metal wires.

Loofah looked at the paper. "That's what the radar's picking up!?" he asked. The arm quickly created a picture of an enormous shark coming toward their submarine. The device drew the sub as tiny in comparison to the shark.

"Sharks can sense blood from a long ways away," Eerey informed. "The shark must smell Guy's blood and came back."

"It's big!" Edict exclaimed. "It could swallow us whole!"

Eerey burst Edict's hopeful fantasy with her reply. "No, it could eat us a little at a time. The sub would get stuck in its throat."

"The hull will protect us," Loofah stated.

Eerey prepared to break this little pair of rose-colored glasses, although she would prefer not to. "Given time, those teeth could slice the hull. If it's hungry, it could continue to spit out the metal until it found the meatier morsels inside this can of sardines."

"I'm not a sardine!" Loofah protested.

Edict shook his head in agreement. "No, you're not. Still, you do offer the most food out of all of us for a hungry giant shark. It won't matter, because we'll drown before that."

During the conversation, the talking gorillas prepared to fire the air-driven torpedo tube.

"Wasn't Eightball nesting in the tube?" Edict asked. The gorilla captain prepared to pull the lever.

Eerey's eyes grew wide. "Don't!" she pleaded. The gorilla pulled the lever. They watched the dark water as Eerey's bowling-ball-sized pet spider burst from the torpedo tube and headed for the giant teeth. The white, figure-eight symbol on the spider's belly grew rapidly smaller. Eightball, with his extremely tough skin, headed for the shark teeth.

Eerey wiped a tear as she watched her beloved, enormous, and possibly poisonous pet spider disappear into the inky blackness. She turned a dark expression to the talking gorilla. "I hope you aimed for its nose at least. Eightball doesn't deserve to die for no good reason."

The gorilla blinked its black eyes at her.

"Wow," Edict whispered to Loofah, "those talking gorillas sure are surly."

"I don't know about that," Loofah said, "but how do we know they actually talk? I've never heard them say a word!"

Edict shrugged. "Mister Cryptic called them 'talking gorillas'. He told our parents we'd be safe with them if we had to take the sub."

Loofah examined the back of one of the gorillas from a distance. "I hope Mister Cryptic was right. They're the only ones who know how to run the sub."

Eerey paid no attention to the conversation. Instead, she watched the pen furiously portray the radar readings. It drew a picture, showing the decreasing distance between the shark and the submarine. It showed a small dot meant to be Eightball.

Eerey nodded with satisfaction. "Eightball's going to hit the shark right on the nose!"

Loofah rolled his eyes. "So what? It'd be like being hit on the nose with a bb gun!"

"I was shot in the nose with a bb gun once," Edict offered. "It hurt like the Chuck Dickens!"

"Shark's hate being hit in the nose too," Eerey said. "It might just scare him off."

The mechanical arm ripped away the top sheet. It started to draw Eightball hitting the shark in the nose. The next picture had the shark veering sharply and swimming away.

"Ah!" Loofah exclaimed. "It's leaving!"

"Yeah," Edict nodded. "Let's hope it doesn't come after us again."

Eerey watched the radar device as it tore off another sheet and began scribbling furiously. "It might not have been coming after us after all…"

"What do you mean?" Loofah demanded. He looked at the picture the machine drew. He became mesmerized by it.

Edict nudged between Eerey and Loofah. "What? What are you looking at?" Edict gasped as he saw the unfinished drawing. It depicted a gigantic squid, with its arrowhead-shaped body. Long tentacles streamed behind it. In all, it was easily as long as the shark and looked far longer. They looked out the front bubble ports. They could see the creature removing the distance between it and the sub. It glowed with beautiful blue lights flashing around its body and down its tentacles. Eerey let out a breath at the terrible beauty of the creature.

"Well," Edict said, "it could be worse. At least the shark's gone."

Loofah watched as a tentacle shot out and began wrapping itself around the ship. Brilliant blue lights flashed down the Squid's enormous appendage and illuminating the control room. "Oh yeah," Loofah said. This could be much, much worse."

Chapter 11
GIANT GLOWING TENTACLES

Nobody breathed as the long tentacles wrapped around the ship. One enormous tentacle, flashing its blue light like a police car, covered the front windows. Eerey allowed a gasp to escape her lips. "It's impossible," she said quietly. "I know certain deep-sea cuttlefish glow, but a squid this size has never been seen. Megaladon sharks have been reported before, but never confirmed."

"What about giant squids?" Edict asked.

Eerey nodded. "They've been reported and remains found of giant squids...nothing this big, though. The biggest found was about 66 feet. And nothing that glows like this one. The bio-luminescence is amazing. I can't believe this occurred naturally."

"Bio-luminescence?" Edict said. "What's that?"

Eerey rolled her eyes. "It glows in the dark."

Edict smiled. "Oh yeah! Just like the lichen in the caves at the Cryptoid Zoo! This is weird, though."

"Weird things occur naturally," Loofah replied. "Like orangutaurs and hairy brats."

"Maybe something or someone created this," Edict said. "Maybe orangutaurs don't occur naturally either."

Loofah laughed, but fell quiet as the enormous eye of the squid moved over the portal.

"That's a HUGE eye," Edict interjected with respectful awe. "I think that eye's bigger than our homework table at home, Eerey!"

Eerey nodded at the suggestion. The round eye seemed to examine them through the glass. Perfectly round, the eye stared for a minute. Its light-blue surface surrounded a round, black iris the size of a car tire. The squid rolled its tentacles around the surface of the Aunt Alice like constrictors coiling around a prey. The eye fell backwards to reveal the squid's razor-sharp beak.

"It's going to eat us!" Edict exclaimed. Eerey and Loofah stepped backwards, watching the horrendous beak draw the bulbous glass window between it. This offered a front-row view of the beast's dark maw. Tentacles constricted about the vessel. The squid pulled at the metal. The iron walls groaned.

Eerey clenched her teeth. "It will lose interest once it has a taste of iron, but it can certainly destroy the ship!"

"Can it squeeze the sub like a soda can?" Edict asked.

Eerey shook her head. "It's not squeezing, it's pulling the ship apart!"

"That doesn't sound good," Loofah mumbled.

"It doesn't sound good for good reason," Eerey said. "The Aunt Alice can probably withstand any pressure put on it by the squid. It's designed for deep-sea trips. But if it tries to pull it open like a giant clam, that's when there will be problems. We need to make it forget the ship as a meal, and pretty soon!"

Edict scratched his head. "I don't have my watch, but I think 'pretty soon' has come and gone."

The squid clenched its beak into the bulbous window. It caused a slight fracture around each of the sharp points, but it stopped at just a firm grip on the protruding glass 'eye' of Aunt Alice.

"We can't stand around looking at our watches," Loofah said. "Besides-some of us don't have watches. We've got to do something!"

"What can we do?" asked Guy.

The ship groaned in reply as it tilted to the side and sent all of them all tumbling against the wall. The iron hull began to fail. Rivets popped out of the seams and water trickled in.

"There's just one thing to do," Eerey sighed. "We've got to let Pen out."

Her companions had just one question. "What!?"

Chapter III

BETWEEN THE DOPPELGANGER AND THE DEEP BLUE SEA

Eerey rushed back to her room. She pulled her backpack from under the furniture piled against the wall. Passing one of the gorillas in the hallway, she hurried back to the control room.

Edict looked at her as she rushed in. "Are you really going to let Pen out?"

Eerey opened the backpack and pulled out a vial with a shiny point of light floating inside. "What if I am? Just trust me and keep an open mind."

Loofah huffed as he shifted on his hooves to maintain balance. "I really don't like guys that tried to kill me. It's tough to open my mind that far."

Eerey nodded. "I don't like it any more than you. He's really the only one of us," she glanced at the gorillas as they wandered into the room, "the ONLY one of us that has the power to keep this boat afloat! He's a will-o-wisp right now, a being of pure light; but he can turn into anything. We need something that can stop the squid, or we'll lose everything."

Eerey put her hand on the rubber stopper, twisted, and began to pull. "Don't let him out, Eerey!" Guy said. "We're already in enough trouble as it is!"

"Listen Guy," Eerey said, peering at the invisible boy. "We have to." The stopper came loose with a squeak, and the tiny light flew out.

"Stop him!" Edict said as the light flew around the room. "He's getting away!"

"Away to where?" Eerey asked. "If we're trapped in this submarine, so is he!"

The dot flew over to Loofah.

"Shoe fly!" Loofah shouted. He waved hairy paws at the light dot. "Get away from me!"

Loofah struck the will-o-wisp away, but it instantly began to grow and change shape. The light dimmed and disappeared as Pen took on the appearance of Loofah.

"Oho!" Loofah exclaimed. "I don't like that at all!"

Pen, looking exactly like Loofah, grinned. "Try being stuck in a glass vial for a while," he quipped. "I can assure you, you would not like that much either."

Guy tapped his finger on the glass. "Here's the problem, Pen."

With a quick glance, Pen smirked through his faux-orangutaur lips. "There's your problem. I can turn back into a will-o-wisp, and they're water proof."

Eerey nodded. "That may be, but are they deep-sea pressure proof?" The ship lurched as the squid gave it a tug. It tilted downward and started to sink. "I haven't heard of any research. Do you want to take that chance?"

Pen pulled at the whiskers on his chin. "I guess it could be dangerous to assume." He smiled. "Still, it might be fun to see how it all plays out."

Eerey twisted her hair. "I'm not sure you really have the luxury for fun when it comes to dying, do you? I have a proposition. We'll let you go if you get rid of the squid."

Pen laughed at the offer. "Sounds like a poem! But you have already let me go, my dear! It's never easy to put the genie back in the bottle once you let the cat out of the bag."

"That's true," Eerey agreed. "Still, you're in the same sardine can we are and you don't have any DNA left to get out of this mess. I'll trust your more generous nature. I don't think you really are the beast you seem."

"Oh, you don't, do you? Being stuck in a test tube can make one, well-rather testy. I've had a lot of time to think about my 'generous nature' during my incarceration, and how much of a beast I really am." Pen's eyes narrowed. "Any guess as to what my own conclusions were?"

Edict cleared his throat. "I'd guess you're holding a grudge of some kind."

The brow of Pen's orangutaur forehead lifted. "I guess you're the smart one of your party! Why would I help you-besides the goodness of my heart? I can assure you, there is little of the type of 'goodness' you might seek there for salvation."

Eerey laughed. "Salvation? We wouldn't come to you for that! It's not that we don't trust you, which we don't. We really don't think you can even take the squid anyway. You were our last-ditch effort. If we thought you could help us, don't you think we'd have come to you first?"

Through tightened lips and flashing teeth, Pen replied, "Really? You think one oversized piece of calamari is a match for me? Seriously?"

"Seriously," Eerey sneered. "More than a match! More like a butane lighter!"

"Of course, I know what you're trying to do."

"You do?" Loofah asked. "Can you tell the rest of us? Because we have no idea!"

Pen laughed, then explained. "It's entirely simple, you simpleton! If your brain wasn't mostly hair, you might have seen it already. Your friend Eerey is supposing that my ego will get the better of me and I'll dispose of the squid out of rash conceit."

"That would be silly!" Edict interjected.

Pen nodded. "Of course it is. And I'm amazed at how well your cousin knows me. It's as if she can read my mind. I'll do it just to show you how powerful I really am-for all the good it will do you! This ship will sink no matter what I do now. It is well beyond repair or recovery."

"What?" Eerey asked. "Are you going to beat the squid with that frail orangutaur body?"

"Hey!" Loofah objected.

"Forget it, my friend," The fake Loofah said. "She is just trying to goad me more." He turned to Eerey. "It's all so very unnecessary, my dear. I said I would defeat the squid for the sake of my ego. I will do so."

"What can you turn into that will defeat the squid? Have you thought of that?"

"I'll touch the squid and get its DNA, of course!"

"How will you touch the squid?" Eerey smirked. "After all, the water pressure might kill you, in whatever form of creature there is DNA for here."

Pen's eyes widened as he realized she was correct. "Maybe you have some dried fish?" he asked hopefully.

"Maybe," Eerey agreed. "Probably not, though. Most of the edibles on this boat are grown in the dirt."

"What…worms?"

"No," Eerey sighed. "Dried fruits and vegetables, with some grains and nuts."

The ship lurched again. They all moved toward the front as the sub tilted toward the back.

Pen shrugged. "Not unless you have some squid DNA."

Looking about the room, Eerey found herself entirely without a sample of squid DNA. "No, I don't…wait!"

Rushing over to a guttered candle, Eerey pulled off a piece of dripping wax. "Will this do?"

"Does that look like it will do?" Pen growled in frustration.

Eerey nodded. "It does to me."

Chapter IV
MYSTIC WHALE

Pen's ground his teeth so hard he seemed he might break one. "How is a piece of wax candle going to help?"

"Because," Eerey started, "It's likely made of whale tallow, which was pretty common in the 19th century. It could be from a whale called Balaena mysticetus, or Bowhead whale. Let's hope so, because they are fairly large-about 90 feet long. Some of the giant squid's natural enemies are whales."

Reaching for the tallow, Pen smiled. "The DNA should be fresher, but I think that will work after all!"

"That's great!" Loofah chimed in. "But won't the pressure crush you anyway? Mister Cryptic said that your bones and organs are soft while you're changing."

With a shrug, the doppelganger replied. "We'll see if I can take the pressure long enough to change."

"Say," Edict said, "isn't there a mounted swordfish in the captain's quarters? That might be more seaworthy. You could change into that first, and a whale outside."

They all walked back toward the captain's quarters where the gorillas stayed. As they walked down the hallway, the gorillas followed them, grunting and shrieking loudly.

"Don't worry," Eerey assured the primates. "We just need a small piece off the back. It will still look fine."

Pen walked over to the swordfish. The gorillas watched. He peeled off a flaking piece of the fish's skin and showed it to them. "This is all I need," he assured. Satisfied, the gorillas left the room. "Aren't they supposed to be talking gorillas?" Pen asked.

Edict shrugged. "So we've been told."

Guy spoke invisibly. "Do you have everything you need, Pen?"

A smiling nod from Pen. "This will do nicely. Now we need to find a way to get me out of the submarine."

"Already handled," Eerey said. "Follow me."

Eerey walked down the hallway again with the others in tow. Walking to the torpedo cylinder, she began turning the wheel holding the launching space shut. Guy stood next to her, grasped the wheel, and helped her turn it. She smiled slightly at Guy and turned her attention back to the wheel. "Thanks."

The catch unlatched with a *thunk*. Eerey pulled the hatch open, leaving a cylindrical space for a torpedo.

Pen shook his head and waved his hands. "Oh, no-you're not going to shoot me out like a torpedo!"

"This is the best way," Eerey said. "It's air-driven, so you won't get hurt."

"That doesn't sound just a little painful to you?" Pen sighed through his faux-orangutaur lips. He tapped Edict's arm and turned into a perfect copy of the hair-covered boy. "Okay," he said and climbed into the chamber. "Remember-if I survive, I will come back, and I will get you for this."

With that, the perfect replica of Edict turned into the perfect replica of the fish hanging on the wall. Eerey closed the hatch over him. The torpedo tube fired. All turned to look at the three gorillas near the firing lever. The gorillas shrugged in unison.

They looked out the ship to see the swordfish rocketing past the squid and through the water. As it moved, it grew larger and changed shape. The pointed nose widened and flattened. The fins disappeared. The skin darkened and changed to a navy blue until Pen became a gigantic whale. The whale that was Pen turned to the boat, looked at Eerey inside as she peered through the window, and then swam straight up.

Everyone sighed. "I told you we couldn't trust him," Loofah said somberly.

Chapter V
WHALE OF A TALE

The party stood at the front of the control room as the declining angle made it hard to stand elsewhere. Long moments passed. Everyone turned to the Eerey. "What will we do now?" She shook her head at the not-entirely-unexpected betrayal by Pen.

"There is one more thing we might try," Eerey said. Why they looked to her for help, she wasn't sure. The situation seemed hopeless on its face, but underneath it seemed nothing short of a miracle would save them. Eerey started to speak, but stopped as she saw an enormous creature swimming toward the Aunt Alice with a vengeance. "It's him!" She shouted uncontrollably. "He's come back to fight the squid!"

The others laughed with unbridled joy. "I thought he'd left!" Loofah admitted. "I'm glad I was wrong!"

"I just thought of something," Edict chimed in. "Now that he's a whale he probably had to surface to gather air. Isn't that right, Eerey?"

Eerey nodded. "I don't know. It might have just been to make us sweat. I don't care either. As long as he stops the squid!"

In a sweeping motion surprising quick for the whale's enormous bulk, Pen aimed for the squid's arrow-shaped head.

With a violent collision, Pen crashed into the squid's head and knocked it aside. It bounced from side to side like a punching bag, its eyes blinking. The whale swam away and turned around to repeat the strategy.

Though not seriously hurt from the impact, the squid seemed angry. It wasn't likely to allow Pen to repeat the same attack.

The suction cups disengage from the sides of the ship with a slurping sound. The squid swam under the Aunt Alice, trailing its long tentacles behind. Pen swept by the front of the ship.

The faux-whale slowed and waited for the squid to attack him. The squid swam right toward the whale, ignoring the plunging submarine. Pen swam right toward the squid. Eerey thought she could see a snarl in Pen's enormous whale mouth.

The two titans clashed as the boat moved away. The squid used its two main fins to suction-cup the sides of the whale's face, as a doting grandmother might gather the cheeks of a grandchild. To Pen, however, it was not love the squid intended to show.

The whale plunged full-force into the body of the squid and pushed it back through the water. Tentacles wrapped around Pen's massive whale-body as he thrashed and pushed at his foe.

The Aunt Alice continued its decent into the murky waters. Any view of the odd battle slowly disappeared.

Eerey ceased watching the display. "Hurry!" She shouted. The others abandoned their posts at the submarine ports. "We need to get the ship to rise instead of sinking!"

The gorillas already worked to right the ship, pushing buttons and pulling levers with abandon. If it was planned on the part of the gorillas, none could tell. Their actions seemed entirely ineffective. The ship continued to descend despite slight turns of direction here and there.

Loofah lost his patience and went over to the gorillas. "Get away from there! I don't think you guys know what you're doing!"

Edict joined Loofah as the gorillas sulked away. "This looks easy," Edict suggested. "I think even a monkey could do this!"

"Edict!" Eerey objected.

Turning to the gorillas, he apologized. "I'm sorry, I didn't mean…"

"Of course you did!" Loofah interjected as he pulled a lever and the submarine began to ascend. "We don't have time to coddle sore egos! Besides; I'm orangutan, not a monkey! Neither are gorillas! We are all proud simians!"

Eerey nodded as she came over to help interpret the various gauges, wheels and levers used to run the ship. "At least the water isn't leaking into the ship anymore now that the squid isn't pulling it apart at the seams. Once we get it closer to the surface, it will be easier to pilot. Right now, it's pretty damaged and limping along."

As they rose, Eerey saw a flash through the dark water. "What is that?" she asked, but none could see what she saw with her keen vision. The flash came closer, shining through the deep at intervals. When she finally saw what the object she let out a sigh. "Oh, no! This is getting entirely ridiculous!"

"I thought it was already entirely ridiculous!" Guy interjected.

Eerey rushed over to the periscope and focused it. The scope brought the object into closer view. "No," she said, "this is even more ridiculous than before." She moved aside so Guy could have a look.

"It's the shark again!" Guy said in dismay while the enormous predator moved toward the ship. "Can't we just have an ordinary day for once?"

"Ordinary people have ordinary days," Edict shrugged. "We have the kinds of days strange people have."

The massive shark loomed larger and larger as it came closer and closer. It opened its massive jaws as it approached the submarine. The enormous, gaping maw lined with rows of bestial teeth sunk into the side of the ship. The shark's one metal tooth, obviously the work of some deranged sub-aquatic dentist, shined brightly as Aunt Alice once more became prey to a massive underwater monster.

"What's it doing?" Loofah asked. "It can't hope to eat us!"

"It could." Guy shook his head. "Hope springs eternal, you know."

"I'm hoping this rowboat doesn't spring a leak," Edict put in.

"Keep hoping," Eerey replied, "and start thinking of a way out of this. Pen's not here to bail us out this time!"

Chapter VI
THE UNDERWATER ISLAND

The shark began to swim away with the submarine in its jaws. The passengers of the Aunt Alice stood helplessly inside.

"Cut the engines," Eerey suggested. "We obviously can't struggle the ship out of the shark's jaws."

Edict pushed the lever to the 'off' position. The ship fell quiet as the shark glided upward through the water.

"How come it's not trying to rip us apart?" Loofah wondered aloud. "Why isn't it trying to eat the ship here?"

Eerey shrugged.

"Maybe," Guy said with invisible lips, "just maybe he doesn't want to eat us!"

"What else could he want?" Edict wanted to know. "He probably thinks we're just a big fish!"

"He's probably smarter than that," Eerey suggested. "I'm not sure he ever wanted to attack anyone. Even when he sliced Guy's leg, it could have been an accident. After all, he couldn't see you either."

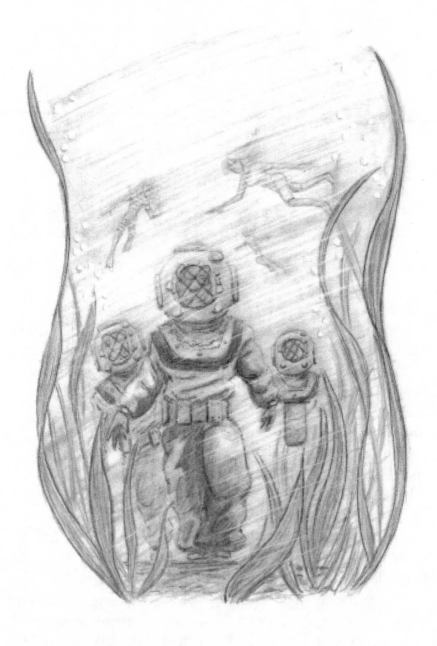

"I wonder why he was running from the squid," Edict mused. "I mean, if Pen as a Bowhead whale could take the squid on, certainly a shark of this size could!"

Eerey nodded. "That's true. Squids have been known to take on predators and eat them. If the shark could get his teeth into the squid, he'd have more than a fighting chance. On the other hand, a squid could wrap around a shark's midsection and avoid the teeth altogether. Those are the shark's only weapons, and the squid's sharp beak could make quite a meal of shark flesh."

"Well," Loofah said, "if the shark's not going to try and eat us, and I'm not sure it won't, where is it taking us?"

"Unless we can figure out a way to get him to let us go," Eerey replied, "we'll just have to wait and see where he takes us."

The idea didn't seem entirely reasonable to the rest of the party. Still, they didn't have any better ideas. They sat down and waited.

After some time the shark carried the submarine to the top of an underwater mountain. They could again see the surging waves above them. The waning sunlight came to them through the filter of seawater.

As the shark crested the mountain peak, the occupants of the submarine saw people with green skin swimming and playing. The people had webbed feet and hands, and wore black-and-white striped swimming clothes that came to their elbows on the shirt and knees on the pants.

A forest of purple reeds grew in hollow, four-foot, inch-thick strands. It swayed with the gentle current. Streams of bubbles came from the ends of the reeds. The people occasionally stopped to breathe the bubbles from the reeds before continuing their frolics.

"Are they…" Guy started.

"It looks like it," Eerey replied. "They're using the air from those plants to breath underwater."

"Are those plants making oxygen?" Edict asked.

"They must be," Eerey replied. "Very fast, too."

With a huff, Loofah let his opinion be known. "That's dumb! No plant that can produce oxygen that fast."

"None that we know of," Edict agreed. "I've never seen anything like these plants or these people."

As they debated, the shark let go of the submarine without ceremony and swam away. Unguided and powerless, the Aunt Alice landed gently in the silt.

"Now we're on the side of the mountain," Guy remarked.

"I'd like to go speak to those people," Eerey said.

Guy looked up the slope. "Do we swim up there?"

Edict shook his head. "No. We take those diving outfits from the diving chamber. I don't want to rely on those reeds for breathing. It might only work for them and not us."

"I'll stay here," Loofah replied. "Those diving suits are only designed for bipeds anyway. I'm more than just an orangutan, you know."

The four went to the room where suits hung from hooks in the wall. The shape of the waterproof suits shared an outline with humans. Eerey wondered if the design seemed suitable for anything living. The round, brass helmets gleamed as they sat on a shelf. Industrial rivets thrust out from the spheres. Small, round windows rested at the front and top of each of the metal bubbles. Brass canisters hung over the neck to carry the breathing air pumped into the helmet.

Eerey took a suit and helmet into another room to change in private. She appeared moments later to meet the suited Guy and Edict in the hallway. Guy's invisibility caused his suit to disappear, but not his helmet and air canister.

"Why isn't your helmet invisible?" Edict's words were muffled by the enormous helmet he wore.

"I have a hard time making metals or glass invisible," Guy explained. "This helmet is pretty big. "It's tough enough to carry this thing without trying to make it invisible too."

Eerey returned and entered the pressurized room with her cousin and the invisible boy. About the size of a large closet, the metal room felt tiny once Loofah shut the door and spun the wheeled handle to lock them inside. Loofah looked through the door's round window. Edict gave him the thumbs up.

Water seeped into the diving chamber. Edict checked the latches on his suit. Guy, now a disembodied brass helmet and air canister to all appearances, paced back and forth. The water filled the chamber and submerged the three figures. Eerey spun a wheel in the wall. A door sprung open to the outside. The three figures stepped out onto the ocean floor, their weighted boots sinking into the sand.

Eerey pointed upward and started to walk toward the peak with its forest of purple reeds and swimming green people. The metallic soles of the boots proved heavy and difficult in the water, but their weight kept the divers from simply floating to the surface.

"These are diving suits?" Edict shouted. "They should call them sinking suits!" Neither Guy nor Eerey could make out what he said.

Looking at the Aunt Alice, they could see Loofah's smiling face through a round port. Their slow, clumsy stumbling seemed to amuse him. Edict suspected all the ribbing the orangutaur would offer when they returned.

Breathing in the stale, metallic air loaded into the canisters decades ago, they continued their climb. They entered the mass of reeds growing down the slope. Eerey took her helmet off, despite frantic hand-waves from Guy and Edict. She breathed in some bubbles from a reed and smiled. It was pure oxygen. She tried to get the others to take their helmets off, but they pointed behind her. She turned around and saw her first green human up close.

The handsome boy swam up to them cautiously, his blue eyes in marked contrast to his light green skin. He smiled pleasantly beneath his long, dark-green hair. Eerey nodded her helmet up and down. If she said anything he wouldn't be able to hear her, so she said nothing.

The boy waved his hand to indicate he wanted them to follow him. They followed him slowly as he swam away. In a short distance, they walked among a crowd of the underwater people. The people swam slowly by the group. They looked and spoke to one another and pointed at them. Their speech barely audible through the helmet, but not clear enough to understand. The boy stopped to converse with some of them.

All of the people had the same dark green hair and light green skin as the boy. One of the girls said something to the boy, and he displayed his teeth in a laugh. The teeth appeared to be quite normal, if a little thicker than those of regular humans. The boy gestured again and they all followed.

The reeds slowed Eerey up as the stalks wrapped around their legs. The underwater people followed along as Eerey's party trudged through the tangled plants. The green people swam around the suited youths and gesturing to each other. Eerey, Edict, and Guy walked through the ruins of a crumbled city toward a tall tower made of black rock. The rubble of bricks from the ruins rested in small piles covered with moss. Only crumbling portions of a few walls and broken doorways remained.

The boy swam to the door of the tower and opened it, inviting the three to follow. The cut stones of the tower proved to be in good condition. The door led to a round room illuminated by electric lights behind a ceiling of waterproof glass.

Chapter VII
ISLAND QUEEN

Walking through the door, the party gazed about. The boy shut the door and pulled a lever in the wall. The water drained through a grating in the floor. "Where are we?" Eerey asked the boy. "And who are you?"

"You're on Kanute Island," the boy replied in perfect English. "My name is Godwin, and I am the prince of Kanute Island. If you will allow, I will take you to my sister, Queen Maurine. She rules this land and can answer all your questions."

Carrying their helmets under their arm, the three followed the boy through a door he opened in the wall. They descended a stairwell spiraling downward. Lights brightened the stairs as they descended.

At the bottom of the stairs, a level floor spread out. Walls made of tan rock made an irregular room about the size of a convenience store. Aside from the stairs, the room held only a large door in the wall. This Godwin opened and directed them through. Blue lights illuminated the large, domed room they entered. Inlaid in the floor were straight squid legs hewn in gold that radiated from the middle of the round room. They joined a

throne designed as the body of the squid of solid gold, its pointed head creating the back of a seat while ornate tentacles twisted together created a base.

On the throne rested a beautiful young woman with the green skin and hair common to the underwater people the group had seen already. She wore a long dress made of a shiny blue material. "Greetings travelers," she said with a pleasant smile. "I see you have met my brother Godwin. "My name is Queen Maurine. What brings you to Kanute Island?"

"A giant shark with a metal tooth," Guy blurted before blushing. He quickly added, "Your majesty."

"You are referring to Rover." She smiled. "He landed on Kanute Island with a terrible toothache. The infection nearly killed him. He stayed docile enough to allow our dentist to repair the tooth and give him antibiotics. We trained him while he healed."

"You mean like a dog?" Guy asked.

Maurine stood to her full height. She stood well over six-and-a-half feet tall in her intimidating stance. She nodded lightly. "Much as you might train a dog, yes." She looked at the helmet floating in the air. "I must object to your remaining invisible in my presence."

"I apologize, your majesty," Guy said as he bowed. "I cannot become visible, but you can see where I am by the helmet floating in the air and hear my position from the light buzzing sound. I always buzz in the light. The brighter the light, the louder I buzz."

Maurine rolled her eyes. "I suppose that will have to do for the moment, since you must remain invisible."

"I don't understand," Eerey said. "Why we have been brought here?"

Maurine laughed at the thought. "You? You have not been brought here! We need the Aunt Alice. Our diplomacy with the

Ottermen has…fallen into disarray. We stand at the verge of war, and we need the submarine to stave off an attack from Kraken. We did not expect it to have a crew."

"The Kraken?" Eerey replied. "The giant sea monster that attacked ships?"

Maurine nodded. "There isn't a single Kraken, as no species long survives without others of its kind. The Ottermen have captured a Kraken and intend to use it to garner control of Kanute Island."

"Perhaps, Maurine," Godwin interrupted, "that a brief overview of our history might help matters."

Godwin turned to the visiting trio. "You see, King Canute sent an exploratory vessel from England in 1025 to search for new lands. About twenty people came on that particular journey, prepared to start a colony loyal to the King.

"The ship struck the top of the black tower outside. It jutted just slightly above water then. Over the last ten centuries the island has sunk further, and the tower no longer reaches the surface of the ocean.

"After striking the tower, it became clear the boat would succumb to the violent waves and sink. The people aboard retreated to the one piece of solid area as refuge-they climbed onto the tower. There, they found a door and upon opening it discovered the tower was waterproof and dry inside. They descended the winding stairs and huddled at the bottom of the tower.

"With the meager provisions they managed to salvage, the explorers knew they could not last long. Over the next few days the men caught fish from the top of the tower, which the women prepared below for an unappetizing meal.

"One of the men named Eadric went fishing one day and fell into the water. Too exhausted to swim, he sank to the ocean bottom. As he was losing consciousness, he observed the bubbles coming from the reeds outside. Desperately, he attempted to breathe the air produced by the bubbles. He found the air was pure and allowed him to breathe the bubbles produced by the plants. He also bit a piece of the plant off and found it to be sweet as honey and extremely edible.

"After some time to recover, he swam back to the top of the tower and climbed back inside to inform the others. In a few days, they made accommodations to recover reserves from their sunken ship that lay in the forest of reeds. Fresh water became the most important. They gathered casks of it to the tower using the reeds to assist.

"Of course, this newfound ability to survive gave them no serious chance to continue their journey. As time went on they adapted, and even began to enjoy their new way of life. They overcame the fresh water issue as they became accustomed to the ocean. They dubbed the island Kanute Island and claimed it for England. Unfortunately, there was no way to benefit as a colony, but it has thrived as a community to the present day. Although we are an English colony, we have had no great need to tell England or anyone else for that matter about our presence."

"That's amazing!" Edict said once it seemed Godwin's narrative was complete.

"Amazing!?" Eerey snickered. "More like unbelievable! You expect us to believe a ship struck a submerged tower in the middle of nowhere by accident? That's too much of a coincidence."

Godwin nodded. "Ah, yes! People of today have a disdain for fate, and prefer to call it coincidence! We Kanutians suppose that our people were meant to discover the tower." He shrugged. "Call it coincidence if it comforts you."

"More likely, you built the tower yourself!" Eerey retorted. "The island has since sunk and placed it under the ocean surface, that's all."

"Ah!" Godwin laughed. "A very convenient scenario you have created to explain everything! I assume the existence of the plants fits in as nicely?"

Eerey rolled her eyes. "Undiscovered life forms are no great feat to explain. There are thousands of new insects discovered all the time. Science doesn't know everything yet."

"Be that as it may, let me assure you that we did not build the tower or any of the structures on this island. After the first Kanutians created a working lifestyle, the newly-created leisure time allowed exploration inside the tower. They discovered the doorway we came through, for instance, and this room as well as the city you have not seen yet."

"There's more?" Guy asked. "This room is cool enough!"

"If you didn't create this…" Eerey started.

"We cannot be certain who created it," Godwin replied. "There are so many sunken mysteries it is difficult to guess what this one may be. Could it be the sunken continent of Atlantis? It certainly could, but it is not necessarily."

"Why haven't you been found yet?" Edict broke in. "There are plenty of devices and satellites that can find many hidden things."

Maurine nodded. "Yes, but that's usually only if people are looking for it. Besides, a lot of the technology we helped design; at least some of us who went to the surface for schooling. It is not so difficult to trick a computer when you understand it well enough."

"You go to school on the surface?" Eerey asked. "What about your appearance?"

"A little makeup," Godwin assured, "can hide our green skin from discovery. Our webbed hands and feet do not prove extremely difficult since we remain fairly unsocial while on the surface. It is embarrassing, but we must admit distrust for those who do not share our appearance."

"You see," Maurine continued, "extended exposure to the air and food from the reeds turns the skin of humans green. Generations have lived underwater, and we have even started to be able to breathe both surface air and to grow gills. We have become semi-amphibious, although we still rely on the reeds when convenient."

Godwin nodded. "The internet makes it so we hardly need to go to the surface to learn about the technology anyway. We can learn all we need to keep detection devices from discovering us. Anything we need manufactured is of little consequence as well, since we can salvage untold wealth from shipwrecks on the ocean bottom."

"Still," Maurine sighed, "all is not perfect here on the island. The Ottermen want Kanute Island, and the greedier of them are willing to war for it. Like humans, the Ottermen are air breathers. The forest of reeds would allow them to stay under water longer as it does us. They hope to create a base from which they can steal technology from those on the surface. They recently salvaged a sunken nuclear submarine. With its technology they can keep the surface hostage. The island would give them an excellent base from which to exploit the entire world."

Godwin nodded. "Our sources inform us they plan an attack on the island soon using the Kraken. We needed the Aunt Alice to stave off the Kraken."

"Why would they use the Kraken," Guy wondered allowed, "if they have their own submarine?"

"The Kraken can burrow in the dirt," Maurine replied, "and weaken the foundation of the island."

"How did you know about the Aunt Alice anyway, and how did you know we'd be driving it?"

"We had sent out Rover in hopes of finding it. He can sniff out more than just blood. That you were aboard is unexpected, as we supposed it may have sunk. There is no record of it we have found on the internet.

"The inventor of the Aunt Alice stopped by during the 1880s. The encounter is recorded in our history. The construction of the ship's hull included material and technology far ahead of its time. It can dive deeper than most modern submarines. Unfortunately, the inventor and his crew escaped."

"Escaped?" Guy asked.

Maurine nodded. "We couldn't very well let him return to the surface world knowing what he knew of Kanute Island if we wanted to keep it a secret."

"How can you let us go, then?" Edict asked.

"Good question," Maurine held her chin. "I hope the answer is obvious."

"What do you mean?" Edict asked again.

Maurine walked toward them, her face a serene smile. "It means we cannot let you leave."

"Maurine, no!" Godwin objected. A door in the side of the room opened. Several underwater men carrying tridents strode toward them.

"It's the only way, Godwin," Maurine replied. "We have to take them as prisoners." She turned to the leader of the underwater soldiers. "Ignatius, did you search the Aunt Alice?"

Ignatius nodded and looked out the door they had entered. He waved his hand to the soldiers outside. "The craft is in remarkable state of preservation. We found this."

Carrying a helmet under his arm, Loofah came into the room, pressed forward by two armed soldiers. Water dripped off his hair and covered the ground around him.

"Loofah!" Edict exclaimed.

The orangutaur shrugged in reply. "I guess it's back to the cages for us, pal."

"No," Maurine said. "No crude cages for you. You will be our guests in the island, and treated to all the comforts of our home."

"Yes," Eerey nodded, "but not all the comforts of our home. We have family and friends. You know-lives."

"You will have your lives here," Maurine assured. "You will have your friends too. You might even make new ones."

"Yes!" Edict smiled at Maurine. "It won't be so bad, Eerey. I'm your family, too!"

Eerey rolled her eyes. "Small compensation there," she huffed.

"Come now," Maurine said. "It can be pleasant if you like." She lowered her eyes to the floor. "Or unpleasant if you prefer. I will leave it to your own choice."

"If I get a vote," Loofah said, "I prefer pleasant!"

"Well Miss Eerey..." Maurine waited.

"Tocsin," Eerey replied. "It doesn't matter what you know. We can't stay."

Maurine shrugged and turned her back. "It's your choice if you prefer it unpleasant."

"No," Eerey interrupted. "I just prefer freedom."

Maurine walked to the back of the round chamber. An ornate door inlayed with gold patterns swung open. "Let me show you what we have to offer."

The trident-wielding underwater soldiers urged the party to follow. They all gasped at what they saw.

Chapter VIII
SUBTERRANIAN SUBMARINE CITY

The door opened into a large cavern. The green roots of the reed forest above covered the ceiling and rock walls. A staircase made entirely of mother-of-pearl wound down to a small town constructed of tightly-knit coral reef blocks. Antique streetlights illuminated the avenues, separated by channels of water instead of streets. Rowboats made their way up and down the avenues instead of cars. Four bridges formed a square connecting the blocks of houses at each intersection. The water reflected green light that danced on the buildings and walls. It reminded Eerey of Venice.

"It's awesome!" Edict announced.

"It's wonderous!" Loofah agreed.

"It's not bad," Eerey replied. "Looks like nice place to visit."

Maurine laughed, "You might even want to live here! There are few complaints."

"I have one to register," Eerey said. "Where's the complaint department?"

"We don't even get enough for a separate department," Maurine assured. "You might try the waste disposal office. Or, you can register it with me." She smiled. "I do have a little pull, being Queen and all."

"You are my complaint," Eerey retorted. "I don't like being imprisoned, no matter how pretty the lobster trap."

"It is out of my hands," Maurine replied. "I wish we could let you return, but we cannot guarantee you would not reveal the existence of the island. Can you guarantee that beyond any doubt?"

"Yes," Eerey replied. She glanced over at Edict and Loofah. No Guy? She wondered where he had gone, but said nothing. She looked at Edict, a bright grin escaping his hair-covered face. "I can guarantee that I won't reveal anything, but I honestly can't speak for my friends."

Maurine nodded. "It is settled, then. The four of you…" She halted mid-sentence. Looking to the top of the stairs, she saw Guy's helmet and air canisters neatly abandoned on the landing. Her eyes narrowed as she examined the three of them. "Where is the invisible one?" The three offered an honestly confused shrug.

Maurine turned to the leader of the soldiers. "Find him Ignatius!"

Ignatius took the men up the steps with a hurried wave of his hand. Maurine called back, "just three of you!"

Ignatius pointed to two of the men and waved the rest back. "The rest of you, take their breathing apparatus!"

The six men remaining took the helmets and air canisters from Eerey, Edict, and Loofah.

"There," Maurine smiled. "Does it feel as if a weight has been lifted of your shoulders? Now you can enjoy yourselves."

"Maurine," Godwin addressed his sister. "Can we try to figure out a way to give our guests the freedom they so obviously desire?"

Maurine sighed. "You know I would like that as much as they. Unfortunately, their freedom could spell doom for Kanute Island. As queen, my first duty is to protect my subjects and their homes. I'm sorry, but I won't risk the lives of hundreds of Kanutians for the convenience of three strangers. They will have to remain, held by force if necessary, until we can arrange a more suitable situation.

"That will have to wait until after we have dealt with the rogue Ottermen. I hope you can see the quandary we face dear brother."

Godwin looked at the three and nodded. "There is no obvious conclusion to the matter."

Maurine clapped her hands together. "I am pleased you agree. Perhaps you would be so good as to offer our guests a tour of the town."

Godwin nodded. "Good," his sister said and walked back up the stairs. The door clanged shut with the finality of prison bars. Godwin looked at the three and smiled. "We may as well make the best of it. I'm certain you will find the town distracting at least."

Godwin's words rang true in Eerey's ears, and his voice soothed her concerns. She was thankful for the respite from her thoughts, but two concerns remained foremost in her mind. Where did Guy disappear to and what happened to Eightball?

Chapter IX

WHERE GUY DISAPPEARED TO AND WHAT HAPPENED TO EIGHTBALL

Carrying the helmet and the air canisters around made Guy tired. He took them off while Maurine talked to the others on the staircase. She looked up and saw he wasn't wearing them anymore, and ordered her soldiers to find him. He hadn't gone anywhere, but she'd assumed he had.

As his pursuers rushed past, Guy simply joined in unseen. He looked down and took note that the lead lining of boots showed. They were placed there so divers could walk underwater without floating to the surface. He slipped out of them as Maurine gave the order to send Ignatius with just two of the men. Now without any large pieces of metal on him, Guy turned

entirely invisible. He went with Ignatius and the other three as they rushed off to search for him.

Ignatius went first to the open door in the throne room through which the soldiers arrived. They entered a brightly-lit corridor. Guy started to buzz loudly, but he ducked into the shadows of a doorway. The soldiers didn't seem to notice the sound. Ignatius shouted orders loudly and the men listened and obeyed his every word. One soldier looked directly into the doorway where Guy stood, but saw nothing. The soldier moved away to continue the search.

The soldiers moved down the hallway. Ignatius barked orders The soldiers replied with, "yes, sir!" and "No sir!"

Guy ventured into the hallway and followed them at a distance so his buzzing might remain unnoticed, despite the increased volume that came with the increase of brightness.

As Guy followed, he heard a noise behind him. The entry door opened and three more Kanutians entered. Two carried a metal box as they followed the third. Guy ducked into the shadows again until the newcomers passed. The group caught up with Ignatius and crew.

"What are you doing here, Flora?" Ignatius asked the leading Kanutian.

"We discovered something extraordinary on the Aunt Alice," Flora replied. Her hair resembled Maurine's, although not as long. "We brought it back to dissect it. What are you doing?"

"We're searching for an invisible boy," Ignatius replied. "Let us know if you see him. It's imperative to the safety of the island."

"Isn't that obvious?" Flora huffed.

Ignatius nodded. "It is to a soldier." He smiled at Flora. "What are you doing later?"

Flora laughed. "Some things aren't so obvious to a soldier, are they Ignatius? I'm dissecting this specimen; now-and later."

"What is it?"

"It's a spider we found outside the ship's hull. I've never seen the like before. It's about the size of a tea kettle. It took some doing but we managed to capture it without being bit. It could be venomous. We don't know yet."

Guy listened intently to Flora's words. They must have found Eightball! Maybe the spider kept a string of webbing attached to the Aunt Alice and followed it back.

Ignatius' party continued their search as Flora's group walked on. Guy used their shadows to hide as he followed right behind them in the hallway, keeping the light and thus the buzzing tones he emitted to a minimum. Their lively conversation distracted them from the light buzzing, and Guy began to suspect all the Kanutians had a mild case of 'swimmer's ear' and didn't hear extremely well at any rate.

After a short journey they entered a dingy laboratory. The Kanutians set the box on a stainless steel table and backed away. The lid to the box fell open and Eightball clattered onto the tabletop. He crawled around the table as the Kanutians kept their distance. Guy moved into the shadows to watch.

"Get it restrained," Flora ordered. Her two cohorts circled the table with strips of cloth. The spider spun in circles to keep his eyes on them.

Guy wondered what to do. He couldn't let them dissect Eightball, could he? Eerey talked about how tough the spider's skin was. Perhaps they didn't have instruments to penetrate the shell.

Flora moved over to a cabinet and opened it. "I'll prepare the laser drill." She pulled out a complex device. It looked fairly convincing. Guy drew in a breath and moved to the table.

One of the Kanutians lunged for Eightball while the other distracted the spider. Eightball spun rapidly and growled, causing the attacker to back away. The other moved to grab him, but the spider suddenly disappeared.

"Whoa!" the Kanutian said as he backed away.

"What is it?" Flora demanded.

"The specimen," the man replied, "it disappeared!"

"Disappeared?" Flora repeated the last word.

Nod. "It was there, Flora. It just turned invisible!"

Flora smiled. "That's another matter altogether. If it disappeared, that's a problem. If it's just invisible, it's still in the room and we can find it."

"How will we know if it's still here?"

Flora moved over to the cabinet again and pulled out an odd set of glasses with telescoping lenses and wires around the frame. "With the infra-red goggles."

When Guy heard this, he didn't wait. He pushed the hallway door open as he carried Eightball under his arm like a football. He didn't know if the spider was visible using infrared, but Guy knew he was warm-blooded.

"Someone just ran out the door!" Flora informed, the glasses still in her hand. "It must have been that invisible boy Ignatius is looking for! After him! Quickly!"

The two men each grabbed a spear-gun and rushed out the door while Flora fastened the strange glasses to her head.

Guy ran down a hallway. He buzzed loudly under the harsh glaring light. Hearing the obnoxious buzzing, Flora pointed down the hallway. "After him!" she commanded.

Guy ran as fast as he could. He felt lucky that his pursuers were not likely to injure him. That feeling whizzed past him as his pursuers fired a spear gun.

"You moron!" Flora admonished. "Why are you shooting!?"

"I'm shooting at the boy!" the man returned.

"You can't see him!" She shouted, her face turning red. She pulled the glasses off and threw them to the floor. "I can't see him either! He doesn't even show up on infra-red! Keep following the sound, but we don't want to kill him! We're scientists-not soldiers!"

The trio moved after Guy. He managed to make progress while Flora discussed the issue with her comrades. Guy ran down hallway after hallway, now entirely lost in the confusing maze of doors and branching corridors. He couldn't shake them, and the scant shadows offered in the doorways wouldn't keep him from buzzing.

Looking down a short hallway, Guy saw an elevator. He rushed to it and pushed both the buttons on the panel. His pursuers came around the corner as the door opened and he slipped inside.

"Stop him!" Flora shouted. A spear whistled toward Guy. The doors closed on it with a *thud* and held it there.

Flora put her hands on her hips. "Well," she sighed, "at least he won't be a problem anymore."

Guy didn't breathe until the elevator was moving. He hadn't noticed which button he pushed in the elevator.

The spear moved to the top of the elevator and the roof pressed on it until it fell to the floor. The doors slid aside to reveal the darkened shore of a cave with a blue grotto. Dim yellow lights reflected off the water, and Guy left the elevator. In the near-darkness, he buzzed hardly at all. He doubted his pursuers would find him here.

The rock walls and sandy shore reminded him of the cave with the chameleon crocodile. At that point, his friends helped him out. He shuddered as he thought of being all alone in the dark.

The water traveled away from Guy and disappeared where it met the darkness of the cavern. A thumping, drumming sound came from the gently lapping water. It grew louder. Something agitated the water with washing-machine swirls.

The sounds worried Guy. He didn't want to see what came from the black liquid. Better to face infrared lenses and spear guns than what he didn't know. He rushed over to push the button on the elevator, but found none. The rhythmic sound beat time with his heartbeat.

Guy turned back to the water, attempting to remain perfectly still. He clutched Eightball to his chest like a teddy bear. The spider responded by wrapping its arms around Guy's chest.

The sound grew louder and louder as whatever created it approached the surface. Holding his breath, Guy resisted the urge to close his eyes and face whatever came at him.

Suddenly, the water bulged and rushed over the shore. It engulfed the invisible boy and his arachnid package. The wave swept Guy and Eightball into the pond, or lake, or ocean. Which, Guy could not tell due to the darkness. He soon fought for his life under the water. Invisibility failed to protect him from the blind water as it tried to fill his lungs. He managed to swim to the surface and steal a breath of air before sinking again. Guy could not swim, with or without the enormous spider attached to his chest.

He surfaced once again to a horrifying vision. A giant, red lobster-claw the size of a truck rushed at him, pinchers spread. Before Guy could react, the claw grasped him in its clutches. His lungs compressed as the pincers squeezed his chest. While in mortal danger, this point is a good time to leave Guy to his adventures and return to him and Eightball at some point in the near future.

Chapter X
STREETS OF KANUTE CITY

Eerey and Edict strolled with Loofah and Godwin down the sidewalk next to the lazy river flowing between the blocks. Children leapt into the water and swam beneath it surface, playing and splashing each the other. Rowboats glided past, their green-skinned navigators staring with black irises at the group, mouths agape.

"Don't mind them," Godwin remarked. "They are naturally suspicious of people who do not look like them. They have never been to the surface world to converse with 'regular' people. If they had," Godwin laughed, "they would have more reason to suspect humans of sinister motives."

"Not all humans," Eerey reminded. "Not even most, as far as I can tell. I'll bet you not all Kanutians can be trusted either. Isn't that true, Godwin?"

Godwin shrugged. "You will find the city of Kanute and the people who dwell here unlike any on the surface."

"I know what it's like to be unlike," Eerey replied. "It hasn't hurt me much."

Loofah sniffed the air loudly. "It smells down here," he noted. "A little like an indoor swimming pool."

"I think it's you Loofah," Edict quipped.

"I got wet when they brought me here," the orangutaur admitted. "It is humid down here though. It smells like the shore of the ocean."

"It is extremely humid down here," Godwin replied. "It will take some getting used to." He looked at Eerey and offered a shy smile. "You will get used to it, though. We have everything here that you have on the surface. What we do not have, we can get. It is really a nice place to live."

"It is a nice place." Eerey admitted. "To visit. Can you show us one of the houses?"

"I can do better than show you just any house," Godwin said. "I can show you your house. We have one specially prepared for you, Eerey."

"Me?" Eerey questioned. "Why just for me?"

"Well, not just for you. Your friends are to share a different house of their own."

Godwin led them over a bridge and down the sidewalk on the other side. "Here we are," he announced upon coming to a structure made entirely of coral. The building's walls were deep crimson and purple.

"How do you construct these with coral?" Eerey wanted to know.

Godwin nodded. "We use genetically-engineered coral to grow the houses complete, and in the open air. We arrange the DNA to take any shape we want. In this case, we made it the shape of a living space."

"That's impossible!" Loofah snorted.

"Yes," Godwin agreed, "but the proof, as they say, is in the pudding. This house was grown right on the spot." He turned to Eerey. "This will be yours."

"While we are visiting," Eerey reminded.

"It will be a long visit," Godwin replied. "That, I can promise you. Once you get used to it, you will not wish to leave anyway."

Edict smiled as he looked at the structure. "Show us our house!"

"In good time," Godwin replied. He went to the door and opened it. The door seemed like an ordinary door, but it looked alien against the coral. Bowing, he waved his hands toward the interior. "Eerey, if you will…"

"If I must, you mean." Eerey retorted. She walked past Godwin and into the house.

Eerey let out a gasp as she entered the darkly-colored room. Illuminated by lantern fish resting in glass globes of water, the one-room house proved spacious; and dim. Eerey enjoyed the lack of light in the room, as too much bright light hurt her eyes. The various colors of the coral glinted from the walls. Branches of white coral extended from the back wall, perfect for hanging jackets and clothes. A series of shallow, round holes grew in the walls with planks of wood hammered into them to serve as shelves. Eerey moved over to the shelves to examine the old books and gewgaws decorating them.

"We have not had time to prepare the electricity in here yet," Godwin announced. "The shelves are not yet designed to grow in a perfectly square configuration, but our scientists are working on that. They are already growing square watermelons on the surface world. In the meantime, putting a shelf in them suffices and does not harm the structure. Our science is ahead of yours. We have had more time to study nature by avoiding the wars and diseases."

"It can't be always easy down here," Loofah said.

Godwin shook his head. "Not at all. It's extremely difficult at times, and we do catch whirling-fish disease or some other sickness on occasion. There are plenty of germs and microbes in the ocean. We have occasional fights with other creatures as well—some intelligent and some just hungry. Still, improving our world offers more benefit than wasting our resources fighting. We have avoided involving ourselves with the surface world for that reason."

"Where do people shop?" Edict inquired.

Godwin nodded. "We have stores down here with adequate shopping for food and clothing. Our submarines go to the surface world regularly, and much can be ordered online. We live a peaceful, quiet existence." The prince shrugged. "That is, of course, ignoring our current conflict with the greedy Ottermen."

A booming sound punctuated Godwin's sentence. A group of Ottermen rushed down the street, spear guns in hand. They had the general size and look of average humans. The main difference rested in their seal-shaped heads and the fine, oily fur coating their bodies. Long whiskers thrust out from their top lips. If it wasn't for the deadly spear guns they carried it would be easy to mistakenly call them 'cute'. Before the group could react, the Ottermen surrounded them.

"Speak of the devils," Godwin gasped. He raised his hands as the lead Otterman threatened him with a spear gun. "Well, well—if it isn't Shellwalker."

The head Otterman nodded, his toothy smile crawling like a cockroach across his lips. "It is indeed, Prince Godwin. It is too long since we last talked old friend."

"Well, Shell," Godwin retorted, "how should we rectify the issue? I cannot speak if you spear me to death."

The Ottermen laughed in concerted *arf* *arf* barks. Shell composed himself. "Nothing so dramatic, please! We are taking you prisoner."

Godwin seemed surprised. "Just I?"

Shell nodded as he looked over at Godwin's companions. "Just you, my liege. These others are of little use to us." He waved his hand dismissively. "Shoot them all."

"That doesn't sound good," Loofah said as the Ottermen surrounded them threateningly.

"You know what to do," Edict said. He raised his fists.

Godwin leapt in front of the threatening spear guns. "I will not have you kill the girl I love!" His face turned beet-red.

Shell rubbed his chin. "Fine. We'll kill you too."

The young girl's features remained placid at Godwin's surprising admission. "Thanks for the gesture, Romero."

Godwin's blush darkened. "Don't you mean Romeo?"

"If that's what I meant," Eerey replied, "that's what I would have said."

With amazing quickness, she pushed him aside and grasped the spear gun out of the closest Otterman's hand. He moved back in surprise as the others rushed forward.

Eerey spun, her white dress dancing inches above the pavement as she fired the spear gun into the next Otterman's weapon. The dislodged gun clattered over the sidewalk. Eerey's red hair sliced the air as she leapt at it. She rolled as she grabbed the gun. Leaping to her feet, she prepared to fire the newly acquired weapon.

The Ottermen decided to leave rather than face the young hellion. Seeing their retreat, Eerey dropped the weapon.

Edict walked over and stood next to his cousin. "Eerey, I didn't know you knew martial arts! That was just like out of a karate movie! I thought you just stayed in the dark and read all the time. How did you learn how to do that?"

Eerey shrugged. "I stayed in the dark and read about martial arts."

Loofah objected. "You can't learn martial arts just by reading!"

Eerey raised an eyebrow. "I can't? How do you know?"

A loud, rhythmic sound filled the air behind her. Loofah let out a gasp as Godwin ran to stand next to Eerey. All three of them looked at something beyond her. Edict's mouth gaped wide as Eerey spun to look at the giant lobster about thirty feet long that moved toward them. Its legs beat a rhythm against the coral pavement.

"Cool!" Edict said, incongruously. As the gargantuan lobster stood there, holding the invisible Guy Guess trapped in one of its claws, Eerey could think of many things it was. Cool didn't come to mind.

"You know what we need now?" Loofah asked. "We need a big, boiling pot of water and a large stick of butter. I saw it in a movie once where they fought a giant crab."

"I don't like shellfish," Eerey replied.

The retreated Ottermen returned, rearmed with new spear guns. Shell laughed as he came closer. "Well, Godwin. I don't suppose you have anything to say? Perhaps you will thrust yourself between your girlfriend and the grinding claws of death?"

"I'm not his girlfriend," Eerey said.

Godwin said nothing to Shell or Eerey. He gaped at the kraken.

Shell smiled. "No? I thought not. That being the case, I will take you and your friends as my guests."

Chapter XI
CAPTIVES OF THE OTTERMEN

The trip only took a few minutes, or just a few hours; perhaps more than a day or two. Eerey had no idea, since she slept through the entire ordeal. When Shell said he would take them prisoner, Eerey prepared her stance to fight the weapons from their hands once more. At that moment, the giant lobster called a Kraken by the Ottermen breathed out a green-colored gas. It filled the area, creating an thick cloud even Eerey's keen vision couldn't penetrate. She coughed and grew dizzy. She tried to move, but she stumbled and fell unconscious.

She remembered nothing more until awakening in a cage. The thick bamboo bars stayed fast as iron, as Loofah displayed by pulling violently on the bars of his cage across the cave. Light bulbs hung from wires and illuminated the rough-hewn, moss-ridden walls of the cavern. Eerey looked about at the other cages. Loofah continued to pull at the bars of his bamboo cage, trying violently to dislodge them. Edict swung off the bars of the roof of his cage, swinging like an angry monkey. Godwin sat sullenly on the floor, twirling around a pool of water in the sand with a stick.

"Godwin," Eerey said. The prince looked up. "Where are we? What's going on?"

The prince shrugged. "The Ottermen want to use me as a bargaining chip, and to keep me in line by keeping you in your cage. My admission of my feelings," he turned away and crimson, "made you valuable to them. I am so sorry."

Eerey waved the idea away. "Forget it. Let's concentrate on how to get out of here. Safely." She turned to Edict's cage. "Edict, what are you doing?"

Edict smiled and hung with his legs wrapped around one of the bamboo poles in the roof. "Exercising. What else is there to do in an eight-foot square room?"

Eerey shrugged. "Perhaps get Loofah to settle down? His throwing a tantrum really isn't helping."

"Tantrum!?" Loofah stopped pulling at the bars and bared his teeth. "You think this is a tantrum? Let me tell you what it is- it is not a tantrum!"

"That's what it is not," Eerey replied. "That's not what it is. What is it?"

Loofah smiled. "Aha!" he said. "I'm glad you asked! It's an escape plan!"

"An escape plan?" Godwin asked. "How is that an escape plan?"

"I came up with it," Loofah said. "An orangutaur's plan always works eventually."

"What is it supposed to do?"

Loofah offered the prince a patient look. "Help us escape, of course!"

"How will it do that?"

Loofah gritted his teeth. "It just will," he said. "Trust me."

"Perhaps we should think of a backup plan," Eerey suggested. "Just in case."

Loofah snorted. "Okay, you go ahead and waste your time!" He stifled a chuckle. Loofah forgot his amusement upon seeing Shell enter the room.

Shell walked to Godwin's cage. "How is my old friend?" The Otterman jingled keys on a large ring.

"Extremely displeased," Godwin replied. "I will see that this does not end well for you."

The Otterman laughed in barking tones. "You may not live to see how it ends."

"I think you might be surprised," a voice surprised Shell with a reply from behind. Shell turned to see where the voice came from, but Loofah struck him a powerful blow on the cheek.

Edict's eyes widened to see Loofah free from his cage and the unconscious Shell on the floor. "How did you get out, Loofah?"

Removing the ring of keys from the unconscious Otterman, Loofah headed toward Edict's cage. "I told you, you need to trust me." He winked as the door opened. "An orangutaur's plan always works eventually."

The prostrate Shell awoke and leapt to his feet. The Otterman ran away before anyone could catch him.

Edict said, "I guess they don't always work perfectly."

"I never said they did," Loofah rushed after Shell as Edict performed an amazing bound to catch the Otterman. Shell moved too fast. He disappeared into the darkness of a small cave before they could catch him.

Loofah looked at Edict. "You're the expert cave spelunker. You follow him."

Edict shook his head. "Not on your life."

Loofah unlocked Eerey's cage before unlocking Godwin's.

Godwin brushed off his jacket. "We will see more of Shell and the Ottermen. They will not rest until they control Kanute Island."

Loofah held up a hand. "Do you hear that?"

They all listened. A loud scrapping and tapping came from the large cave opening at the far end of the cavern. Eerey peered into the opening with her uncanny ability to peer in the dark, seeing what no one else could see.

"It's the Kraken," Eerey said, "and it's moving fast!"

Soon, the enormous lobster filled the cave opening. It found the group with its eyes and skittered across the ground at breakneck speed toward them.

"Run!" Loofah forcibly recommended. They ran.

Loofah took the lead, with Edict close behind. Eerey and Godwin followed.

"The Kraken doesn't have Guy in his claws," Eerey noted. "It did the last time we saw it."

Godwin shrugged. "Since Guy is invisible, I did not see him either time. If you do not see him, he must have gotten away somehow."

Loofah ran past the others. "That's how I hope we get away-somehow!"

"We won't get away by talking about it," Edict said. "The Kraken won't be able to follow us in here!" He rushed into a cave-mouth about six feet in diameter.

"Wait for me!" Loofah said as he rushed after Edict.

Godwin and Eerey followed behind the orangutaur. Godwin halted for a moment as the gigantic lobster rushed after them. "I can't see anything!" the prince exclaimed. "I'm afraid of the dark!"

Eerey grabbed his hand and pulled him forward. "I can see in the dark," she said. "Hold onto my hand and don't let go. We'll get through this together."

Godwin held Eerey's hand tightly as she ran after Loofah, who stumbled through the dark passage. "Go left, Loofah!" She shouted as she saw Edict take a turn down the passage leading to his left. "Stay with Edict!"

The Kraken reached the cave entrance Edict chose as an exit. The giant crustacean collapsed its armored body to fit through the narrow opening. Eerey watched as it slowly but surely began its journey through the cave walls.

Eerey pulled Godwin's arm with increased urgency. She turned the corner behind Edict and saw her cousin and Loofah blindly examining a cave wall with their fingers. They could not see in the dim light. Eerey, however, saw clearly. The wall was solid and offered no escape!

The Kraken scraped the rough-hewn cave walls behind them in slow but relentless pursuit. Eerey remained silent as the only one aware of their situation's hopelessness. With the Kraken behind them and a wall in front, the party definitely found themselves between a rock and a hard place.

Chapter XII
A PAIR OF NOT-SO-GREAT ESCAPES

The Kraken pressed its stony shell into the cave. The passage of the beast made a horrendous scraping noise against the natural walls that hurt the ears of its prey.

Eerey still held onto Godwin's hand. "There doesn't seem to be a way out!" Godwin whispered.

Eerey shook her head. "There's always a way out. We just have to find it." She looked around in the darkness. "What does this lever do?" As we all know, one should find out first what a lever does before pulling it. Eerey knew full-well this general guideline, and pulled the lever anyway.

A net made of metal rope surrounded the group as the cave filled with water. The netting pulled them upward through a shaft in the rock above them. Godwin exclaimed, "It's a fishing net!"

"So that's what the lever does," Eerey said. She nodded approvingly.

"Why'd you pull it if you didn't know?" Loofah asked. "It could have been something to kill us!"

Eerey shrugged. "The Kraken seemed as if it might kill us," she said. "I figured six-of-one, and at worst, a half-dozen of another. All things being equal, it could not do more harm than the Kraken."

Edict nodded. "I trust my cousin."

"I trust her too," Loofah said. "I'm just worried that being in a fishing-net might not be a good thing."

"Better here than in the belly of the Kraken," Eerey replied. It didn't take long for the net to complete its journey. When it did, it unceremoniously dumped the group onto a sidewalk on the outskirts of Kanute City.

"How did we get back here?" Edict wondered aloud.

"Yes," a female voice replied as they stood to their feet. They looked up to see Queen Maurine, dressed in an elaborate, jade-colored gown. Five soldiers stood by her. "I have a better question-how did you escape the city?" Maurine waved her arm. The sleeve of her gown glided through the air as she pointed at the group. "Seize them!"

Queen Maurine strode away as the soldiers aimed their tridents at the group. "On your feet!" Ignatius demanded.

Eerey shouted after the queen. "Maurine! What are you going to do with us?"

Maurine paused and turned. "You will address me as queen and show proper respect!"

Eerey adjusted her sunglasses. "You've never acted like this before. Why are you angry?"

"I have offered you as many accommodations as possible!" the queen said. "You show disrespect by attempting to leave?"

Prince Godwin stepped forward. "We did not leave sister. The Ottermen kidnapped us!"

Maurine nodded. "You were seen leaving with the Otterman, Shellwalker." Her voice lost some of its anger. "I know you want to protect your girlfriend, Godwin. It is only natural. You do not have to lie to me."

Godwin protested. "I am not lying." The rest of the party nodded in agreement.

"And I'm not his girlfriend," Eerey added.

Loofah struck the pavement with his front hoof. "The Ottermen did kidnap us! Everything he says is true!"

Edict nodded. "Didn't anyone notice the giant lobster or the Ottermen come into town?"

"Yes," Maurine agreed. "It does not mean that they came at anything beside your behest! All of this conflict arose right before you arrived. It may not be coincidence."

"But it is a coincidence," Eerey replied. "It's not so unreasonable to think so."

"It is not," Maurine said. "It is unreasonable to risk the city and its citizens."

"I can vouch for them," Godwin said.

Maurine shook her head. "I do not have the luxury of taking even your word, brother. Your judgment is clouded by your feelings for the girl. Take them away!"

"What will you do with them?" Godwin asked.

"They must remain in the dungeon until I have considered the matter. You must do the same, Godwin."

Maurine turned and walked away. Godwin protested, but to no avail. The soldiers took charge of Godwin and the group. They escorted them into an elevator. Once everyone was inside the elevator, it descended.

"I'm getting sick of this!" Eerey said quietly to Godwin. "All we want is to find my parents and go home! People keep trying to keep us prisoner."

Godwin nodded. "It will get better."

When the elevator opened, it came to the same room with the same cages they recently escaped.

"What is going on here?" Edict demanded. "This is where the Ottermen kept us prisoner!"

"Quiet you!" The leader of the soldiers ordered. "Making up stories won't help now!" He laughed as the other soldiers opened the cages. "Ottermen using our dungeon without us knowing? Preposterous!"

The soldier put the prisoners in individual cages, secured the locks, and left.

"I don't understand what's going on," Edict said.

Godwin nodded. "I think I do."

"What?" Edict asked.

The prince's jaw stiffened. "It is my sister. She is using the Ottermen to get me out of the way."

"Why?" Eerey asked. "She's already queen."

"True," Godwin said, "but she and I co-rule Kanute Island. The people would not stand for it if she became sole ruler without good explanation. It was she who first disclosed the plans of the Ottermen, and it increased her power greatly. She, of course, needed the aid of the Ottermen to carry out her plans. She never counted on us escaping the dungeon, or at least not my escape. That is why she was so angry, and how she happened to be standing there when we ended up in the street of the city."

"What will she do with us?" Loofah asked.

Godwin looked at the orangutaur. "Can you do whatever you did before to escape, Loofah?"

Loofah shook his head. "That was a one-trick pony." He kicked the bars with his front hoof. "We'll have to figure out something else."

"What did you do the first time?" Eerey asked.

Loofah just shook his head.

"Forget that," a voice came from nowhere to their ears. "I'll get you out."

Eerey smiled. "Guy! How did you escape the Kraken?" She could see the invisible boy walking toward the cages with a handful of keys and the eight-pound spider hanging onto his left shoulder. "Eightball! I thought he was gone for good! Where did you find him?"

Guy shook his head. "I promise I will tell you about it after I get you out." He put a key into Godwin's cage. It didn't work, so he tried another. After a few tries, the lock clicked. Soon, he had all the cages open.

"Follow me," Guy said. "I've found a passage to a safe place." He began walking, forgetting only Eerey could see him. Eerey followed him and the rest went along.

Guy led Eerey into a descending cave. The rest followed. Seashells and fish-bones of various sizes and colors covered the sandy, sloped floor. Someone clearly used this cave as a community area. It hadn't been used that way for quite some time.

After they'd descended for about twenty minutes, Guy slowed his pace. "I have something to tell you all," he said as they walked, "especially Edict and Eerey."

Edict smoothed the hair on his hands. "Why us?"

"Because I found another dungeon in a lower cave."

"Still," Eerey said, "why does it concern us?"

"I'll let you decide." The others followed the invisible boy into a vast cavern. Glowing stalactites hung from the ceiling. A shore of sand encircled a large, dark lake. Young Krakens about sixteen-feet-long wandered around the shore a hundred yards off or so. Guy pointed across the lake to some cages.

Eerey peered across the stygian waters. Edict tugged at her sleeve. "Is that?"

Eerey nodded. "Mom…dad…Mister Cryptic!"

"Who?" Godwin asked as he looked at the three figures in the cage. "Are those your parents? How did they get here?"

Eerey looked at the dark waters. With concentration and her uncanny ability to see in the dark, she saw through the murky depths. Far below the surface rested the Aunt Alice next to a newer submarine. She looked away and toward the krakens wandering around the shore. "I'm not worried about how they got here," she replied. "How are we going to get them out?"

"However we do it," Loofah said, "or whatever we do, we'd better do it quick!" He pointed at a group of the krakens headed toward them, opening and closing their claws to create a cacophony of clacking sounds.

"We can't get to them now!" Godwin exclaimed.

Edict growled. "We can. We will. We must!"

"Easy for you to combine auxiliary verbs and pronouns," Godwin replied. "It is going to be harder to get to them! We need to do that first."

"No need to swear," Loofah said. "I've got an idea."

Eerey adjusted her sunglasses. "Let us know your plan this time."

Loofah nodded. "Yep." He turned and ran to the water.

"What are you doing!?" Guy shouted as Loofah leapt in and began dog-paddling toward the cage.

"Lobsters can't swim!" he shouted.

Eerey leapt into the water and swam after him. "Yes they can!"

"Oh." Loofah turned to see the krakens sliding into the water. "I thought they walked on the bottom!"

"They can swim if they want to," Eerey said. The krakens swam backwards, their backs to him. Loofah turned and kept swimming as the others entered the water.

Chapter XIII

OUT OF THE FRYING PAN, INTO THE LOBSTER POT

The krakens entered the water a little ways down the beach, giving the group the advantage of distance. The others caught up with the slower-moving Loofah. "What are you guys doing? They'll catch me, but you could get away!"

"We don't leave our friends behind," Guy replied invisibly from the wake of water he created.

Loofah nodded. "What are you doing, Godwin? We're not friends yet."

Godwin shrugged in between strokes. "Maybe I hope the future is different."

Edict glanced over his shoulder. The water behind them boiled frantically with the giant crustaceans gaining on them. "I hope there is a future!"

Eerey swam next to Loofah. The others, swimming faster, passed them both. "Gah!" Eerey shouted, looking over her shoulder. "They're right behind us! What'll we do?"

"Keep moving!" Godwin said.

"No," Eerey replied. "I've got a better idea." She stopped swimming and floated in the water. Pulling her backpack open, she reached in. Eightball stuck his spider-legs out, but Eerey pushed him aside. She pulled out the rope weaved by Loofah when he and Edict tried to escape the cages at the Cryptoid Zoo.

"What are you doing, Eerey?" Guy asked.

"Keep swimming!" Eerey created a lasso from the rope as the lead kraken approached. She threw the lasso around the kraken's 'neck' and pulled it taut.

The enormous lobster slammed its back into her. She put her hand under the rope and hung on. The kraken thrashed to dislodge her, but she hung on for dear life. Luckily, it did not think of diving. She spat saltwater out of her mouth, being dunked more than once.

The other krakens continued to follow their leader, despite Eerey being astride it. The kraken she rode seemed to forget her and its pursuit through the water. It dove quickly into the water. The rope twisted around Eerey's hand. She couldn't get loose from the huge lobster!

Edict saw the kraken dive with his cousin on its back. Guy saw it too. "Eerey!" he exclaimed. He dove, invisibly, into the dark waters.

"I'm going too!" Edict stated as he dove.

The entire group dove, now following the krakens rather than being pursued by them. Godwin swam fast and soon left the others behind. A lifetime under the ocean made him very accomplished in the water. His sight stayed keen in the darkness. The line of krakens dove past them, playing 'follow-the-leader' rather than chasing the young men.

Guy and Edict popped to the surface like a couple of beach balls. Exhausted, they threw themselves on the sandy shore. Edict began to cry as Guy looked set his invisible eyes on the water.

"I can't believe she's gone."

Loofah swam to the shore. "Gone!" he exclaimed. "What happened?"

Edict sat up and sniffed. "Maybe Godwin will save her," he suggested. "He can breathe underwater longer than we can."

Guy nodded. "Let's hope so. She can't breathe underwater longer than we can."

Chapter XIV
EEREY RETURN

Eerey's vision in the darkness began to fail her as she went further into the depths. She vaguely understood it wasn't her vision that failed her, but her mind. She continued to struggle against the rope, but her strength failed too. She needed air.

She remembered nothing more until she woke up in a hospital bed. The green light in the room hurt her eyes until they adjusted. She saw a figure standing by her bed, but couldn't see it clearly.

"I fear I owe you an apology," she heard a voice say. Her eyes adjusted to the light and brought Queen Maurine's features into focus. "I did not want to see you harmed."

Eerey coughed as she sat up. "What happened?"

"You nearly drowned. Godwin rescued you and brought you here to recover. He couldn't save your companions, however."

Eerey coughed again. "Couldn't save them? What do you mean?"

Maurine walked to the window and watched the aquatic life drift past. "Godwin said the young krakens were after your party.

He barely managed to rescue you. He could not see what happened to the others."

Eerey twisted the corner of her pillow. "Are you sure they are…gone?"

Maurine nodded. "Krakens are ruthless creatures. To get away from them would a difficult feat for air breathers."

Finding a pair of slippers next to the bed, Eerey slipped them on. "Incredible things can happen. I'm going to find out what did happen." She stood up, attempted to steady herself, and sat back down.

"You are not in condition yet to do anything," Maurine gently reminded. She brought over a bowl filled with dried reeds like those the people breathed air from. "Eat, and gather your strength. If you eat this, it will refresh you as it has healing properties as well."

Eerey took a small piece of reed in her hand. It didn't look appetizing, but she closed her eyes and tried it anyway. "It's actually pretty good!" She turned her head away from Maurine. "I don't have time to eat. I need to find them!"

Maurine nodded. "You will never find them if you do not have the strength. Once you're better I will send a search party to help you look."

Eerey ate from the bowl as Maurine talked to her. "I want you to know, Eerey, that I have your interests in mind. I know you want to be free, and you will be. The Kanutians must be safe, and that is my priority as Queen."

"Are you sure they'll be safer by not talking to the outside world?" Eerey asked.

Maurine shook her head. "No, but our encounters with others have not been promising in that respect."

Eerey nodded. "I can understand that. I hope you aren't afraid of them because they are different."

Maurine smiled. "We are afraid of them because they are the same. If we thought they were worse than us we would have nothing to fear, because we could feel superior. If we thought they were better than us, we'd have nothing to fear because we would expect them to act better. If they act just like us-that is terrifying!"

The sound of an alarm interrupted the conversation. Ignatius burst into the room. He crossed his arms over his chest and bowed his head to Maurine as a salute. "My Queen. The Ottermen are invading with the Kraken. They have destroyed the warehouse."

Maurine's mouth fell open. "The food supplies!"

Ignatius nodded. "They also cut down the reed forest. The noilets plants are destroyed."

"This is awful! Without noilets, the citizens of Kanute Island will starve!"

Ignatius nodded.

"Isn't there other kinds of food you can eat?" Eerey asked. "You can't just have storehouses of noilets."

"You can eat anything," Maurine replied. "Our lives depend on noilets. We have grown to depend on the plant for our sustenance."

Ignatius broke in. "It's worse than that, my Queen."

Maurine sighed. "What could be worse?"

The door flew open again. Ottermen surged through the door, lead by Shellwalker. "What could be worse is that we've conquered your island as well. Oh, and we have your brother too. Now, we've captured the queen!"

Maurine smiled. "No you haven't. I have the queen!"

With that, Maurine transformed. Eerey gasped at what she saw, as did the Ottermen. "Pen!"

The face of Pen, disguised as Mr. Cryptic nodded. "Yes, Eerey. You knew I would return." He turned to the Ottermen. "Now, perhaps we can make a deal."

Chapter XV
PEN TALKS TOO MUCH

After his initial surprise at seeing Maurine change, Shell spoke to Pen. "What can you offer us? We have already taken away the food supplies of the island. Our victory is ensured!"

Pen nodded. "Yes, you can take over the island. What will you do then? The population needs to be controlled or destroyed, but it's much better to have slaves than graves. I can use Maurine's form to create a trusted figure that the Kanutians will obey."

Shell stared at Pen for a moment before nodding. "We can discuss this further. You could be useful."

Pen nodded his head toward Eerey. "I will take the girl with me. I am...collecting her and her friends. She could foil our plans if she's left in the town."

Shell shrugged. "We have no use for her."

Pen clapped his hands together. "Good! I will keep her indisposed. When I get back we can make plans."

Eerey stood on the hospital bed. "You're not taking me anywhere!"

Pen looked deeply into her eyes. She tried to shut them, but it was too late. "No, Eerey. I will not take you anywhere. I will let you lead."

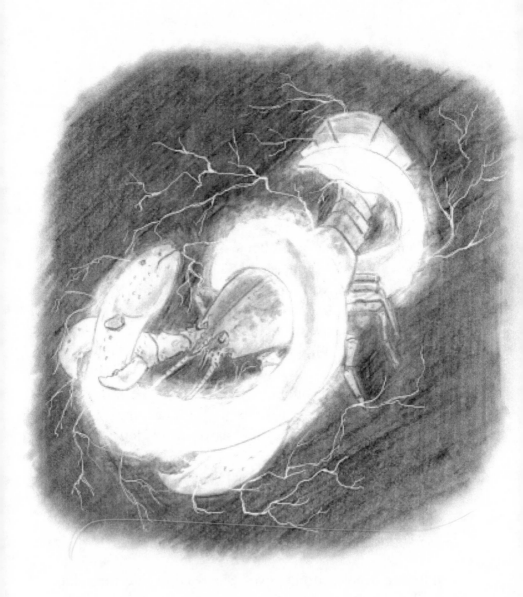

Involuntarily, Eerey stepped off the bed and began walking out the door.

The doppelganger changed again into the form of Queen Maurine and followed Eerey. Pen directed her to walk down the sterile, white hallway decorated with gray doors. The doppelganger gave her single-word commands of 'left', 'right', or 'straight'. Eerey felt compelled to obey.

A green skinned girl her age walked by them in the hallway and said, "hello." Eerey looked at the girl and thought of speaking.

Pen shook his head at her. "There are many ways talking to people could go wrong for you, and far fewer ways they might help. Remember, I'm their trusted leader."

Eerey said nothing. Nobody they passed gave any notice except to give a slight bow of respect to the queen. Eerey walked to an elevator with holes in the door and pushed a button. At Pen's will rather than her own, she stepped into the elevator and pushed the 'down' button.

The door closed. The elevator plunged down. Pen turned back into the figure of Mr. Cryptic. The door opened, illuminating the same beach where Guy encountered the Kraken. Eerey did not know this. The light from the elevator extinguished as the doors slid closed. Though extremely dark, Eerey saw the water lapping on the shore.

"I discovered this spot after swimming to catch up with the Aunt Alice," Pen said. "I see you can speak your mind even when it's controlled. Impressive."

Eerey nodded. "So you beat the giant squid."

"Obviously," Pen smiled. "Only in a sense, though. It wasn't going well, so I touched a passing shrimp and took on its smaller form. I easily slipped out of the tentacles and found a marlin. Sailfish are the fastest known fish–did you know that?"

Eerey nodded.

"Anyway, I followed the Aunt Alice after the shark grabbed it. It was easy to keep up. I watched as it dropped the submarine. I took the form of a Kanutian. I spent time finding out about the events on the island while you were trying to figure out how to leave. It proved no great task to take the shape of the queen. By the way, I told you I could take the squid."

"I knew you could," Eerey replied. "I also knew with your ego you'd have to prove you could."

"I knew that."

"What I don't know, is where the real Maurine is."

Saying nothing, Pen flourished his hand toward the shore. The water bubbled wildly as the Aunt Alice emerged. Through a lit round window, Eerey saw Maurine sitting in a chair. The queen stared blankly out the glass. Behind her sat Loofah and Edict, their eyes glazed. The gorillas moved about in busy motions, but Eerey couldn't tell if they knew what they were doing.

"What have you done to them!?" Eerey demanded. "And where are my parents!?"

Pen looked at them from the corner of his eye. His lips curled into a smile. "Why, my dear! They are all perfectly safe. Your parents aren't here. You can clearly see the others. Do they look injured?"

"No," Eerey admitted. "They are hypnotized!"

Pen nodded. "I knew you were a bright one. They need not stay that way. Uninjured, I mean. Do as I say if you value their health."

Through gritted teeth, Eerey asked, "what do you want?"

"Only your cooperation," Pen replied.

Eerey smiled. "No way."

The reply took Pen back. "What did you say?"

"You can't be trusted! Going along with you puts them in more danger!" Eerey turned to run. She halted as the water began to bubble again. A gigantic claw thrust out from the water and grabbed Pen. The Kraken crawled onto the shore.

"Let me go!" Pen demanded. He turned to Eerey. "Help!" he wheezed. "It's crushing me!"

"Turn into a Kraken!"

"I can't!" Pen huffed. "My bones will be crushed during the change, and the shell doesn't have any live DNA to replicate anyway!"

"That's impossible," Eerey returned. "It must have DNA! Why should I help you? Maybe you can't take the Kraken. I'd like to see if you could stop it or not."

Sweat dripped off Pen's brow. "Okay, little girl. Just remember I told you so!"

Pen groaned as his body turned into green slime. Eerey could hear bones crack during the transformation, but soon enough the Kraken's claw snapped shut forcefully, throwing slime about the shore.

The Kraken turned its attention to Eerey. She rushed over to the elevator door, searching for a button. The juggernaut crustacean followed rapidly on its eight legs.

A giant black eel, a hundred feet long or more, appeared out of the water. It wrapped around the Kraken.

Eerey breathed an uneasy sigh of relief. "Let's see if you're strong enough, Pen!"

The eel hissed as it tightened about the Kraken. The giant lobster reacted by clenching its claws open and shut in an attempt to grasp Pen. Pen let out an electric charge that made the Kraken curl in pain. The electricity in the air caused Eerey's hair to stand up.

"Get it, Pen!" she shouted. "Don't let it get away!"

The Kraken turned and headed back into the water. It managed to grasp the eel with its claws. Pen let out another jolt of blue electricity. The energy crawled over the surface of the water and the outside of the Aunt Alice, making a brilliant display.

The Kraken fell limply in the water and sank into the blackness. Still in its grasp, Pen disappeared with it; apparently unconscious-or worse.

Chapter XVI
TO RESCUE
AN ENEMY

Eerey stood on the shore not sure what to do next. She saw her hypnotized friends standing in the Aunt Alice. She could swim out there and attempt to enter the submarine, but wasn't sure she could get on board.

"What do you think, Eerey?" a voice said. She spun around. Guy stood in the dim light, invisible to most eyes. Eerey could see his outline without a problem.

Eerey smiled. "Guy. I'm so glad to see you! How long have you been here?"

Guy shrugged. "My whole life. Wherever I am, I'm always here."

Eerey laughed. "No, silly! How long have you been on the beach?"

"I've been here long enough to see Pen buy the farm. I followed you from your hospital room. Not close enough that you could hear me buzzing, of course. I've dealt with this elevator before."

"Why didn't you say anything?"

"I wanted to be able to surprise Pen, or anyone else for that matter, if you were in danger. One nice thing about being invisible is nobody knows you're there unless you're careless."

Eerey smoothed her hair. "You were watching out for me?"

Guy nodded. "Friends are supposed to watch out for each other."

"Speaking of friends," Eerey changed the subject, "we need to see if we can help the ones we have. They seem hypnotized."

"I agree. We'll have to dehypnotize them-somehow."

"First things first. We have to get to the Aunt Alice to do that. I can't see how to get over there."

"Simple. Get the apes to bring the ship to us."

"How? I don't even know if they can talk."

"Wait here for me. I've got an idea."

Guy pressed the button hidden at the bottom of the door. The invisible boy disappeared into the elevator. Eerey sat on the shore, staring helplessly at her hypnotized friends. Guy returned after about a half hour, carrying a large bunch of bananas. As long as he held them, they were invisible. When he dropped them on the shore they became visible again.

Eerey offered a golf-clap. "Great idea, Guy! We can make them slip on banana peels!"

"You don't have to be so cynical," Guy suggested.

"No," Eerey agreed. "I don't have to be."

"I found these in the hospital storage room. If we can get the apes to notice, they might come over to pick up the bananas. They loved the dried bananas before we ran out."

Eerey bit her lip. "That is a good idea, Guy. Sorry to make fun."

"That's okay." Guy placed the bananas on the ground and pulled one off the bunch. He threw the banana at the Aunt Alice, hitting one of the round windows.

Eerey clapped her hands. "Nice throw!"

Guy blushed invisibly. "Thanks. I've been practicing for a career in sports. The other team wouldn't see what hit them!"

The pair watched the submarine. The gorilla captain appeared at the window and looked out. Its eyes widened as he saw the bunch of bananas. It began moving its mouth, apparently shouting. Neither Eerey nor Guy heard whether or not it said any words.

The other two gorillas came to windows and saw what excited the captain so much. They all became excited, and soon the Aunt Alice headed for the shore. As it neared, a gangplank fell into the wet sand. The purportedly-talking gorillas rushed out and headed for the bananas. They hooted, hollered, and grunted as they pulled bananas from the bunch. Apparently, none of the sounds they made were words.

Eerey grew impatient as the gorillas ignored her and Guy. "Can you speak, or not?"

One gorilla glanced up from his repast, before grabbing another banana and stuffing his mouth again.

"Never mind," Guy said. He grabbed Eerey's hand. "Let's get on board."

Eerey followed him to the gangplank. The pair walked into the Aunt Alice. They found their hypnotized friends in the control room. Eerey rushed to Edict and grabbed him by the shoulders. "Edict! Edict, wake up! Wake up all of you!"

Tufts of hair fell off Edict's face as she shook him, but he continued to stare forward blankly. She looked at Queen Maurine and Loofah. Neither the pretty ocean-queen nor the orangutaur responded to her pleas.

"They are too deep in a trance," Guy said. "Shaking them or yelling at them won't work."

"What will work then?"

"In the old Svengali movie I saw, only a word from the hypnotist will work."

Eerey's face fell. "But Pen's dead! He can't wake them!"

Guy shrugged. "We just need the word. Only Pen knew what it is. Other than that, we can try guessing…"

"Maybe we could try reading the dictionary," Eerey suggested.

"That might work," Guy agreed. "It might be a word that's not in a dictionary. It might be a word that's not in any language. It might be one Pen made-up."

Eerey sighed and dropped down into a chair. "That could take forever. We can't wait that long."

"Are you sure Pen's dead?" Guy asked. "I mean, I saw him sink too, but maybe he was just unconscious."

"Of course I'm not sure he's dead," Eerey retorted.

"Then, we need to find out if we want to wake them up."

Eerey looked at Edict and Loofah, standing silent and not arguing. "Well…"

"Of course you do!" Guy said.

"I know, I know! Still, how are we supposed to find the Kraken and get Pen back, if it even still has him?"

The gorillas came into the room, towing the uneaten bunch of bananas behind them. "Let's ask these guys."

Eerey turned to the gorillas. "Help us follow the Kraken." Immediately, the gorillas set to pushing buttons and twisting knobs. The engines of the Aunt Alice fired, and the ship began to move. The gorilla captain rushed to the helm and took the wheel. The ship moved away from the shore, then plunged into the black waters.

Chapter XVII
TRAIL OF THE KRAKEN's TAIL

Descending rapidly, the submarine strained under the increasing pressure. Eerey watched as the depth indicator spun around, indicating the fathoms they were from the ocean surface.

One of the sailor gorillas rushed about, lighting candles in little round compartments set in the walls. These shined outside the ship through panes of glass and lit the way. Strange creatures showed in the glow as they swam this way and that. Aunt Alice leveled off as the seafloor came into view.

"How will we find the Kraken?" Guy wondered.

Eerey pointed out the window. "Follow the tail trail," she said. "The Kraken apparently drags its tail as it walks." A long trail in the silt ran along the ocean bottom. Regular dots ran next to it on either side where the Kraken's legs pressed into the mud.

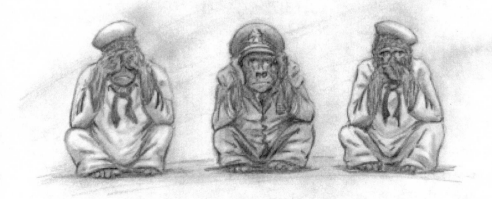

Guy nodded. "Okay, but which direction is it headed?"

Eerey looked at the Kraken's trail and nodded. "The gorillas are going the right way."

"Sure, but how do you know?"

"The Kraken's footprints are dug into the mud opposite the direction it's going," Eerey explained. "It pushes backward to go forward, just like we do. The deep mud shows what direction the prints are pointed."

"What if it's walking backward?"

"It would still have to push in the opposite direction. It's no different either way."

Guy relented. "Okay. I just wanted to be sure."

Eerey looked out one of the front-facing bubble windows. "There it is!"

Guy rushed to the other round window. "Where? I don't see anything."

Eerey pointed out the viewport. "It's right there. It moves fast, too."

Guy squinted and managed to see a dim glow ahead. "I think I see it."

"Oh no," Eerey said. "That's not good."

"What?"

"Look up there!"

Guy looked hard to where Eerey pointed her finger. After searching the dark waters, he said, "Oh. That's not good."

"I just said that."

Guy continued to stare ahead. "I just agreed." Two gargantuan whirlpools glowed unnaturally red as they spun furiously through the ocean depths.

Eerey ran to the gorilla driving the Aunt Alice and demanded, "Turn around! Go back!"

The gorilla tried to turn the wheel, but couldn't. The nearest whirlpool pulled the ship forward. The ship moved faster than before, quickly gaining on the Kraken. As the ship nearly caught up with the juggernaut crustacean, the giant lobster moved forward and leapt into the swirling column. The whirlpool sucked the Kraken in. It disappeared with the whirlpool into a large hole in the ocean floor.

The gorilla captain grunted as it struggled with the wheel, and the two other gorillas came over. All three pulled at the wheel. Their actions resulting in a snapping sound. The gorillas fell to the floor. The captain got up and grabbed the wheel again. It spun freely, but didn't affect the ship's path. He gave up and sat down on the floor.

"What are you doing?" Eerey demanded. "Get control of the ship!" She pointed out the window. "Look at that whirlpool! It will wreck us!"

All three gorillas looked at her. One sailor gorilla put his hands over his ears, effectively blocking out Eerey's demands. The other sailor put his hands over his eyes as the whirlpool came into view. The captain grunted, "Oh no," before putting his hands over his mouth.

"He talked!" Guy said as he pointed at the gorilla captain. Wide-eyed, the latter pressed his hands to his lips harder. "He said 'oh no!'" The captain shook his head. Eerey sighed, "It doesn't matter. If we can't stop Aunt Alice before it's too late, none of us will talk for long!"

It was too late already as the whirlpool sucked the submarine into its swirling tornado of water. Guy and Eerey fell over and hit the wall as the room began to spin. The gorillas remained seated on the floor as the candles flickered. Eerey's hypnotized friends and family tumbled to the floor like broken wooden puppets, their arms and legs placed by gravity rather than choice.

Eerey and Guy sat with their backs to the wall, trying to avoid feeling ill from the spinning of the craft. "What do we do now, Eerey?"

"Hope it doesn't get worse."

As if in reply, Eerey saw the Kraken swim toward their ship, still carrying Pen as the 100-foot electric eel in one of its claws. The other claw opened wide to grab the Aunt Alice. Eerey wondered if the claw could open wide enough to grab the submarine, but stopped wondering when it did just that. The Kraken swam in the maelstrom as easily as a goldfish in a fishbowl.

"Great," Eerey sighed. "We came to rescue Pen, and now we're trapped by the Kraken in a whirlpool!"

Guy shrugged. "Could be worse."

"You really think so?"

"Yeah. The Aunt Alice is holding up pretty well in this whirlpool, and we're still alive. That's something to be grateful for."

"Okay," Eerey nodded. "How long will we be alive?"

Guy shrugged. "I'll be grateful as long as I can. That's all."

"The Kraken could still kill us. Who know what it'll decide to do?"

Guy hit his head with his palm. "I forgot to tell you about the Kraken!"

"What didn't you tell me?" Eerey asked.

"It's not an animal. It's a machine!"

Eerey didn't reply as the deafening noise of power tools filled the air. Eerey covered her ears. Where the Kraken's claw rested against the outside of the ship, the metal began to spark. Saw blades cut a six-foot circle in the hull of the Aunt Alice.

Smoke filled the air as the cut section of the ship clanged to the floor, still glowing at the edges. Guy and Eerey looked at each other with watery eyes as the fumes burnt their nostrils.

As the smoke cleared, Eerey noticed the edges of the Kraken's claw made a watertight seal. A tall figure stepped from a metal staircase inside the claw. Eerey looked quickly out the window to see the giant eel still in the Kraken's other claw. She returned to the figure on the staircase, not knowing what to think.

"I thought…" Guy whispered.

Eerey nodded. "So did I."

Pen, in the guise of Mr. Cryptic, let out a low snort as he walked into the ship. He wore a long black jacket and leaned on a cane. A metal starfish curled into a ball decorated the top of the cane. "You thought," he grinned, "that I was the giant eel floating out there. Actually, that's entirely true. And not entirely true at the same time."

Eerey looked out the window once more to see the eel stir and press its enormous eye to the glass. The eel's eye winked at her.

Pen released a guffaw from his smiling lips. "I suppose I should explain."

Biting her lip, Eerey said, "Yes, you should! First, I demand you undo what you did to our friends!"

Pen shook his head in feigned sadness. "Ah, poor girl-you still do not understand. I did nothing to your friends. No, no." He pointed the tip of the cane out the window. "He did."

Leaning against the wall, Eerey crossed her arms. "Okay. Start explaining!"

Chapter XVIII
SINISTER STARFISH

Guy and Eerey listened intently to Pen's explanation. "You see," he started, "I have had much time to travel the ocean and plan. A fascinating thing about a starfish came to mind."

"A starfish?"

Pen nodded. "Some species can regenerate an entire body from a removed arm. I wondered if it would work if I tried to become a starfish."

Eerey sat down in the captain's chair. "So you became a starfish."

"Yes. Unfortunately, I realized afterward a problem."

Guy repeated Pen's last two words. "A problem?"

Pen nodded. "It was not enough to be a starfish. I had to remove my arms."

Eerey grimaced. "Ouch."

"'Ouch' is right," Pen agreed. "Still, it had to be done. It was not as bad as all that, as I was able to create five of me." He nodded toward the window, "including that fish bait outside.

Unexpectedly, each one is entirely autonomous. It really is like there are five of me."

"I'm impressed," Eerey said.

Pen looked to the roof and adjusted his tie. "How could you not be? The only surprise is you have seemed rather unflappable regarding my abilities until now."

Eerey huffed. "I find your ego the most amazing thing about you so far."

Pen's eyes narrowed as he looked at Eerey. "Do not challenge me," he sneered, "if you want to see your friends again."

"Why can't you bring them out?" Eerey asked.

"As I said before, we're all different." He shrugged and shoved his thumb at the eel outside. "What he did to mesmerize them, I do not know."

"If you're all different," Guy mused, "are you as strong as you were before?"

Pen closed his eyes and struck the wall with his cane. "We will be stronger," he assured. "Then, the five of us will be unstoppable!"

Eerey smiled. "Are you sure?"

Pen laughed through gritted teeth. "Admittedly, it is not entirely a sure thing. It's never been tried before so far as I know."

Eerey pressed Pen. "Will you get jealous of the others? How will your ego handle them being as powerful as you?"

"One thing I can tell you is that I am powerful enough to destroy you!" Pen's body distorted as his legs and arms twisted and changed. His face fell and sunk into his chest as he transformed into a gigantic starfish and started to fill the room.

"Help me get these guys out of this room!" Eerey shouted as the starfish continued to grow. She grabbed the arm of the unconscious Edict and began to pull.

Guy stood next to Loofah's prostrate form and shook his head. "Are you kidding? It'll take too long!"

Looking around the control room, Eerey spotted small metal chest painted white with a red cross on its side. She threw it open and pulled out some vials. An arm of the starfish fell with a loud *bang* and crushed the box as Eerey moved to her mesmerized friends. She handed three vials to Guy. "Here!"

Guy looked at the glass vials as Eerey rushed over to Edict. "What do I do with these?" Guy asked.

Eerey pulled out the rubber stopper and put it under Edict's nose. "This!" Edict coughed and stirred. "These are smelling spirits! They were used to revive people when they fainted!"

Eerey moved over to Loofah, leaving Edict to wake up on his own. "What's going on?"

Guy shook his head as he placed the spirits under Queen Maurine's nose. "No time to explain, Edict! Get to the engine room!"

All of them rushed out of the room with Guy and Eerey prodding on their groggy friends. Eerey rushed into the hallway as one of the starfish's arms tried to grab her. She narrowly avoided it and slammed the door behind her shut. She spun the wheel in the metal door, locking it. Locked out, the starfish arm pressed against the round window in the door.

"What now?" Guy asked.

"What now!?" Loofah broke in. "What is going on in the first place!?"

"Giant killer starfish," Edict grumbled. "What more do you need to know, lamebrain?"

"Hey," Loofah objected. "You don't need to insult me, dunderhead!"

Edict laughed. "Dunderhead!? Who talks like that?"

"I do," Eerey said. "We don't have time for argument. Move!"

Edict started with, "it's not me…"

"Enough!" Queen Maurine said. "Do as Eerey says!"

The queen's forceful tone shut down Edict and Loofah. The sounds of the wheel spinning on the door reached everyone's ears.

"He's trying to get in!" Loofah said.

Edict turned. "He's getting in!" The arms of the starfish, now the size of tree trunks, began sliding into the hallway.

"Let's get it into the engine room," Eerey said as she moved down the hallway. "Maybe it will be too hot for it."

They all moved into the engine room where a metal catwalk encircled the engines and the boiler below. A pair of staircases led down to the boiler and coal stack. One of the sailor gorillas manned the boiler. The gorilla shoveled from the enormous coal pile into the glaring orange fire.

Eerey rushed down the stairs. "It'll be too hot down here!"

Loofah wiped sweat from his brow. "It's too hot up here!"

Edict pushed past the orangutaur. "Stop whining. It should be better than playing Jonah in a giant starfish's belly."

Loofah shrugged, but followed Edict. "I've never tried being eaten by a starfish. You're probably right though."

"Keep moving!" Queen Maurine ordered. "There is no time to discuss the issue!"

Some of the arms of the growing starfish pushed through the door behind them. They reached the bottom of the stairs as the starfish's body squeezed through the doorway.

"Get closer to the furnace!" Eerey said. They all followed her as she moved toward the heat. Ignoring them, the gorilla threw another load of coal into the boiler.

The starfish wrapped its arms around the railings of the catwalk and began to slowly descend, leaving some of its long arms still outside the room.

"Will this work?" Queen Maurine whispered to Eerey.

Staring at the enormous starfish, Eerey replied, "If it doesn't, it won't matter very long." The gorilla continued to shovel coal into the furnace.

Chapter XIX
STARFISH AND STARLIGHT

In the control room, the gorilla captain at the helm twisted the wheel while the starfish grew larger. The starfish pressed at him as it grew, but the pair ignored each other. The gorilla grunted at the annoyance and nothing more. He steered the Aunt Alice toward the whirlpool opposite the one that sucked the submarine down, dragging the attached Kraken/ship with it.

The starfish slid out of the control room altogether with a squishing sound. The gorilla didn't seem to notice its departure at all. The whirlpool's tug pulled the wheel as the gorilla struggled against the whirling current.

The Aunt Alice, with the Kraken as an added burden, struggled forward until the whirlpool sucked it in. The ship began to spin.

The unexpected motion caused turmoil in the engine room. The gorilla in charge of the coal leaned on his shovel to keep from falling over. The rest of the party had no shovels to lean on, and tumbled to the wall. Only Loofah remained standing.

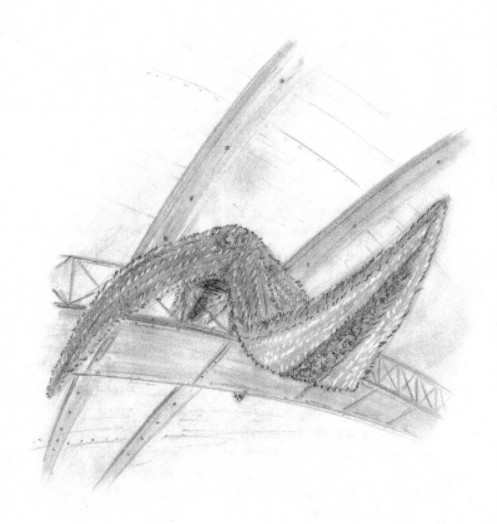

His horseshoes screeched against the metal floor as he slid over it.

Edict stood unsteadily to his feet. "You should get those oiled, Loofah. That sound hurts my ears!"

"Yeah?" the orangutaur replied. "Now you know how I feel every time you're yammering at me!"

"What's going on?" Queen Maurine asked. "The ship's spinning! We must be in a whirlpool!"

"Yes," Eerey agreed. "That's how we got here, but this time we're going up!"

"Whirlpools are naturally supposed to suck things down, aren't they?" Guy asked.

"Maybe it's not a natural whirlpool," Eerey replied. "It might be artificial."

"It doesn't matter," Edict said. "It's pushing the ship up, and we still have a giant starfish after us!"

Everyone looked at the progress of the starfish hanging over the railing. It retracted its arms when they drew near the boiler.

"I didn't think it could take the heat," Eerey said.

His brow dripping with sweat, Loofah leaned against the wall. "That's one thing I agree with it on. I need to get out of here!"

The metal railing buckled under the starfish's weight. With a crash, the starfish and the railing fell to the engine room floor below, pulling the rest of its arms into the room. "Let's move!" Edict urged as he rushed up the stairs.

"You don't have to ask me twice!" Loofah said as he rushed past Edict and began climbing the stairs. "I need a soda!" The orangutaur's horseshoes beat a rhythm against the metal staircase.

The rest of the party followed their lead as the starfish tried to recover from the fall. It began to follow after them before discovering it was too large to avoid the furnace. Instead, it began climbing the wall again, but not fast enough. The group ran above it on the gangplank.

A small arrow shot out of the darkness and hit the starfish's skin. It began to wobble as it continued to struggle upward. Now alone in the room aside from the gorilla, it fell to the ground again. It shrunk and transformed into the form of Mr. Cryptic again. Sweating, Pen stood to his feet. He leaned on his cane as he walked through the engine room. The gorilla glanced at him and shoveled another scoop of coal.

Pen reached the staircase and walked up three steps before passing out and tumbling to the ground.

A figure appeared at the top of the stairs and looked at the doppelganger. "Sorry about that, Pun," The figure who looked like Pen looking like Mister Cryptic but was actually Pan smiled. "You're no longer needed and can go on coffee-break for a bit."

Edict and Loofah rushed into the control room where the gorilla stood calmly at the helm. The ports whirled with dark water. Pinpricks of starlight gleamed through it. Eerey and Guy moved into the room, followed by Queen Maurine. The Aunt Alice spun around the top of the swirling water like a wooden horse on a merry-go-round. The Kraken remained attached by its massive claw. Eerey looked at the stairway to the great 'lobster-chine'.

"Well," Guy said, "we can't stay here. That starfish is going to keep growing!"

Eerey nodded. "We need to go somewhere else."

Edict scratched his hairy head with his hairy arm. "Where else is there, cuz?"

Eerey didn't reply, but headed for the staircase leading to the Kraken. Queen Maurine and Guy followed. Loofah and Edict shrugged at each other. "Might as well," Loofah said. The pair walked after the others.

ChapterXX
INTO THE KRAKEN'S CLAW

Cautiously, Eerey moved up the steps leading into the Kraken. Reaching the top, she looked about the long, football-shaped room. The sound of machinery clicking and spinning filled the room at a nearly uncomfortable level. Several electric lights of various colors blinked on and off in the walls. Wires snaked about the floor. Glass tube fuses glowed inside the open machinery framed by metal boxes.

"I don't see how it's piloted," Guy noted. "There's no chair or steering wheel."

Suspicious, Eerey turned to the invisible boy. "How did you know it was a machine if you'd never seen inside?"

"When it carried me around," Guy said, "I could hear the machinery. I never made it into the shell before."

"If there's no place to steer it," Edict mused, "who's steering it now?"

"I could explain," Pen said, standing at the top of the stairs and leaning on his cane. Loofah and Edict bristled at the doppelganger. "Still, I think I should leave it to the man in charge."

Queen Maurine stepped forward. "Man in charge?" She stepped away and gasped when Pen stepped to the side and Godwin stepped forward. The prince of Kanute Island wore an ornate suit jacket of black decorated with gold paisley designs. A black tie and white shirt beneath complimented his wardrobe nicely. He bowed his head to Queen Maurine respectfully, but his eyes carried malice. "Yes, my dear sister. I am the man in charge."

Eerey started, "Godwin…"

Godwin smiled at Eerey with a softened expression. "Yes, my dear Eerey. I hoped you would not find out this way, but you will forgive me for what you are about to hear. Perhaps not to-day, but we have years for that."

"Enough!" Maurine said. "Explain yourself, brother! What is it to which you refer? Forgive you for what, exactly?"

Pen laughed, but quieted when Godwin shot him a glance. Everyone waited as Godwin began to pace back-and-forth. Fi-nally, he began to speak. "You see, dear sibling, I have waited for this moment. I plan to wrest the throne from you."

Maurine sneered at her brother. "Right when we are strug-gling against the Ottermen!"

Godwin stopped and laughed wickedly. "When you are strug-gling against the Ottermen, sis!"

"I don't understand," Maurine replied.

"The war with the Ottermen is my war against you!" Godwin smiled.

Maurine flushed. "If that is true, Godwin, stop it now before good Kanutians are hurt!"

Godwin shook his head. "I have been away too long for the citizens to trust me right away. They might discover my ambi-tions for the throne. No, dear sister, a throne wrested away in a time of peace leaves the public suspicious that something's not cricket. A loving brother taking the place of a martyred queen during a time of war…well, they will eat that up with sauce!"

"I am still alive Godwin," Maurine reminded. "The Ottermen have not killed me."

Godwin nodded. "That is true. At least, they have not yet. All of that is in the formula."

Maurine frowned. "Yet if the Ottermen war with Kanute Island, they will suffer as well as us. Why would they risk losing a war?"

Godwin laughed again. "I see you do not entirely understand the scheme. The Ottermen we war against are but a few dozen working for me. There is no war to be had with the Ottermen in general. If you were a better diplomat and talked to them once in a while, I would not have been able to convince you of their non-existent threat to us."

"What about us?" Eerey broke in. "We have nothing to do with this!"

Godwin turned to Eerey. "My dear girl, that is true for your friends, and even for the Aunt Alice. I have little use for them, although the submarine will come in handy. You, on the other hand, have everything to do with this Eerey. I saw you first at the Cryptoid Zoo after I hacked into their security cameras. I hoped to find creatures of some use for my ambitions. I must admit a crush at first seeing you. It became part of my plan. If I am to be King of Kanute Island, I will need a Queen. I intend you to be that queen. Using the sunken nuclear submarine as a ruse, I convinced dear Maurine we needed to retrieve the Aunt Alice for that purpose. I retrieved that long ago, and place its workings inside this fossilized Kraken shell. It is now a nuclear Kraken! It responds to my thoughts by computer."

"You have become ensnared in my elaborate netting." A greenish mist began to seep into the room through holes in the ceiling. Everyone aside from Godwin and Pen began to cough as they breathed in the toxic fumes. Eerey struggled to remain conscious as she saw Edict fall asleep and Queen Maurine waver.

Godwin watched as Eerey stumbled against the wall of blinking lights. "You thought, perhaps, that Pen was the reason your friends appeared hypnotized. As I said before, one day you will understand. Pen and I did not arrive at an understanding until recently. We were not even aware of one the other at first. When we discovered mutually beneficial goals, we made a pact."

Eerey watched as Guy and Maurine crumbled to the ground. Loofah fell next, with Eerey laying her head on the soft fur of his horse-back.

"That's it?" Pen asked. "Is that your plan at its end?"

Godwin chuckled. "Hardly, my friend. It is only at its beginning!" The prince's eyes narrowed. Now, we go to war."

Chapter XXI

ATTACK OF THE JUGGERNAUT CRUSTACEAN

The Kraken swam away from the Aunt Alice, leaving it adrift on the water's surface. The gaping hole the nuclear Kraken sliced into it made diving impossible, whatever the gorillas might plan to do.

Diving proved entirely possible for the nuclear Kraken. At Godwin's will, it sank beneath the ocean. Once it reached the seafloor, it began to move along on its eight legs. Its motions propelled it toward Kanute Island.

Inside, Godwin brought his cell phone out of his pocket and dialed. "Shellwalker," he said, "order the attack."

He shut the phone and looked out the windows of the Kraken's round, black eyes. Pen laughed. "I see you have planned well, my young friend."

Godwin gritted his teeth. "Do not confuse youth for inability."

Pen shook his head. "I have done so before with that infernal girl and her friends." He tilted his head toward Eerey. "It cost me dearly. I have learned to not make mistakes any longer."

"What of your starfish clones?" Godwin said. "Did that not become a mistake?"

Pen shrugged. "An experiment I have learned from. Each of them carried ambition close to mine. They now must be destroyed, as I now know they may become my rivals. You took care of one of them in the Aunt Alice. The other is still in the clutches of the Kraken."

"I think not," Godwin said as he looked out the window at the empty claw.

"What!?" Pen shouted as he rushed to the window.

"He slipped the claw while we occupied ourselves with capturing Eerey."

Pen passed it off with a wave of his hand. "No matter. We can deal with him later. I am the center of the starfish, as I kept the main body attached to my leg. The others are weaker than I. Each time one is destroyed his strength returns to me."

Godwin smirked but said nothing as Ottermen with breathing apparatus floated next to the Kraken. Carrying strange rifles in their hands, they swam with the underwater behemoth. Kanute Island, now barren of the vegetation that allowed the Kanutians to breathe under water, came into view. "There she is," Godwin said with pride. "Soon, the island will be mine!"

"How are you going to control the Ottermen?" Pen asked. "They seem unpredictable. Once you are done with the fight, they might turn on you."

Godwin grinned. "Of course they will. However, they are in for a big surprise once the battle is engaged."

"How do you mean?"

"I mean, I do not need the Ottermen as allies. Only Shellwalker knows I am controlling the Kraken. I need the Kanutians to trust and accept me as their king."

"Using deceit to earn the trust of your potential subjects?" Pen rubbed his chin and smiled. "That sounds like it might work!"

"No 'might' about it friend," Godwin assured. "Except the political might I will acquire once my plans are realized."

As they neared the island, a company of Kanutian soldiers swam out, lead by Ignatius. They wore breathing apparatus like the Ottermen and carried spear guns.

Godwin smiled wickedly. "It looks like the movie is about to begin."

Pen nodded. "Let's all go to the lobby and have ourselves some popcorn."

Ignored by Godwin and Pen, the unconscious group of friends began to stir as the smelling salts held under their noses took effect.

Hearing her companions stir, Eerey open her eyes to see a figure standing over her. She shut her eyelids and rubbed them under her sunglasses. The sight was not a welcome one. "What are you doing, Pen?"

"Shhhh!" the figure replied. "I'm not Pen. I'm Pon, one of Pen's starfish clones!"

Eerey sat straight up and looked around. The others appeared to be okay. Edict scratched his furry nose as Loofah stood to his hooves. Through Guy's invisible chest, Eerey examined the room. It appeared to be a simple, metal storage room. Harvested noilets covered the floor in piles.

Eerey looked again at Pon. "If you're not Pen, you're just like him! What do you want?"

Pon shook his head. "I wish you'd keep it down. Yes, I am like Pen-the best part of him. Just because I'm a clone doesn't mean I can't be different."

Slowly, Eerey nodded. "I suppose so."

"Yes, it does!" Loofah said. "A clone is exactly like what it's copied from. That's the point!"

Pon shook his head. "I don't deny that I'm like Pen, but I can change. Don't you think people can change?"

"People can change," Edict broke in. "I'm not sure doppelgangers can."

"That's what doppelgangers do," Pon reminded. "We can change shape. Why not our minds and personalities as well?"

"That's even worse!" Loofah said. "How can we trust someone who can constantly change?"

"Change can be good," Pon said.

Edict nodded. "Sure. It's good if it's for change for ten bucks from a Chasville Gnaw and a Cryptic Cola. It's not good if your airplane turns into a bicycle when you're flying over the ocean."

"Or a mountain," Loofah placed as an addendum.

Edict sneered at the orangutaur. "That goes without saying."

"Then why'd I have to say it?" Loofah asked.

"You didn't."

"Stop it you two," Queen Maurine hissed. "Let's hear…Pon, is it? Let's hear what Pon has to say."

"I believe I'm a better person as Pon than I was as Pen."

"What makes you think so?" Eerey asked.

Pon sighed. "For one thing, I rescued you from Pen and Godwin."

Loofah examined the wall next to him. "Aren't we still in the Kraken?"

"Yes. I misspoke. I am in the process of rescuing you. Dragging you all into the storage room and waking you up was the first step."

"What's the next step?" Loofah asked.

The doppelganger shrugged. "Getting out, I suppose."

Edict smiled. "I'd like to see that!"

A laugh came from the back of the room, causing all to turn. "Yes," Pen said. "I would like to see how you will manage that as well, Pon. Fathoms under the ocean in a craft you do not understand. Worse for you and your friends is that I will stop you!"

Pon clenched his teeth. "Like the way you stopped Pun?"

"Pun had too much of my ego," Pen said, in way of explanation. "It seems you got too much of my good side. His head got too big for him, as it were, when he turned into a starfish. We had to stop him." His eyes narrowed toward Pon. "Now, I will stop you."

"Come on and try!" Pon clenched his fists and stepped forward. "You are stronger Pen. I admit that. I will never stop until you are defeated, because I have your sense of fairness. It is a strong motivator; stronger than your greed!"

Pen stepped toward Pon. "Really? We'll see about that! You play fair. I won't. We'll see who wins!"

A beam of light cut through the air between the identical foes. "Stop!" Godwin demanded, carrying the strange gun used by the Ottermen. "We have no time for this now, and I have a solution. Unless you would like to try the laser beam I perfected for the Ottermen's use." The prince stepped over to Eerey and took her hand. He bowed to kiss it, but Eerey pulled it away in disgust. Guy stepped between Eerey and the prince, though Godwin could not see the invisible boy's defensive posture of Eerey.

Unfazed, Godwin stood tall and smiled. "Madame Tocsin," he began, "you clearly can see there is no escape here. There is no need for this situation. It all revolves around you, my dear." He waved his hand at Edict and Loofah. "Your friends will go unharmed if you will agree to one small favor."

Eerey sneered and clenched her teeth. "What's that?"

Godwin lowered his eyes. "Agree to be my queen."

"No way!" Eerey said. "I'm not marrying you!"

Godwin looked puzzled. "Marry me? Oh dear! That is a long way down the road. I am certain you will like me after the long courtship demanded by Kanutian custom. I am very likable, you know. The courtship takes five years or more. In the meantime, you can sit on the throne in my sister's stead."

"In your sister's stead?" Eerey asked. "Won't she still be the queen?"

Godwin shook his head. "It is no concern of yours."

"She is not going with you!" Pon demanded suddenly. "Is that not clear enough?"

"It is her choice, of course." The prince looked at Eerey. "You can come with me or," he nodded at Loofah and Edict, "your friends will suffer for your obstinacy."

Eerey looked at her hair-covered cousin Edict and the orangutaur.

"Don't do it, cuz," Edict said. "We'll get out of this."

Eerey turned to Godwin. "If you promise you won't hurt Maurine or the others, I'll agree."

Godwin clapped his hands together. "It is done, then!"

Pon stepped to Eerey's side. "Eerey, are you certain you want to do this?"

Eerey nodded. "This is my chance to be a queen!"

Guy dropped his head as he walked away invisibly. "If you really want to go Eerey, we won't stop you."

Chapter XXI
HER EEREY MAJESTY

Ignoring objections from Eerey, Pen spoke with elaborate words and waved his hands in front of Eerey's friends. He placed Loofah, Edict, and Maurine back into a hypnotic state. He tied up Pon before hypnotizing him as well. "I will not harm them," Pen assured, "this time, anyway. The hypnotic gas designed by Godwin is effective, but not so much as straightforward mesmerism."

"What if it doesn't wear off?" Eerey asked.

"It will," Pen assured. "Just not anytime soon."

The battle between the Kanutian soldiers and the Ottermen raged on. With Godwin at the helm, the Kraken rushed into the fray. The gigantic robotic lobster ruthlessly flung aside the Kanutian guard as the Ottermen swam by its side. The battle did not last long. The Ottermen took the battered Kanutian soldiers captives. Godwin drove the Kraken into the cave beneath the island.

Holding Eerey by the arm, Godwin walked down the gang-plank to the dark, sandy shore. Pen followed.

"What about my friends?" Eerey asked.

Godwin turned to the Kraken and looked. "Oh, yes." He re-trieved a cell phone from his pocket and dialed a number. The Kraken immediately came to life and crawled into the water, dis-appearing into the stygian liquid.

"You promised you wouldn't hurt them!"

"Does it look as if they are being hurt?" Godwin asked. "They will remain uninjured."

Pen nodded. "Even though they will remember nothing of the island," the doppelganger assured.

"That would be for the best," Eerey agreed, "but what will they think about me not being around?"

"They will not know you are on the island," Pen replied. "They won't know how to get back here, that's for certain! They will only know that you are happy where you are at and do not want to see them."

"They'll never buy that," Eerey replied.

"They will have no choice. It's not a fire sale, you know."

"Maybe not, but you're still trying to burn them on the deal," Eerey said. "It's not fair, and you know it."

Pen smiled. "Let me know when you find something in life that's fair, dear. I'm only here for me. Doesn't that sound reason-able?"

Eerey nodded. "Yes. Anything can sound reasonable. It doesn't make it any better if it's wrong."

"You're absolutely right. I prefer to be wrong when it's right for me. Why are you going along with Godwin's request? Is it because it's right for you?"

Eerey smirked at the doppelganger. "When else will I get the chance to be a queen and eventually marry a handsome prince? Yes, it helps protect my friends. It's a win-win situation all the way around for me. Godwin agrees to not hurt them and I agree to take advantage of a life of luxury."

Pen stepped back against the wall, his eyes wide. "Eridona Tocsin! I am surprised at you!"

"What? You think you have the lock on selfishness?" Eerey tsked. "I'm surprised at you now, Pen. You can't be so naïve. I have a chance to become rich and famous with very little effort. Can you blame me?"

Pen's features changed to a grin as he eased away from the wall. "Not at all! I would take that opportunity in an instant. I just wish I knew you were so cut-throat all along. It might have saved me some effort."

Godwin climbed into the elevator first, followed by Eerey and Pen. "It is over with my dear. We will arrange for my rule of the island now, after a skirmish with the Ottermen, of course."

The elevator hummed as it rose to open into the sterile hallway traversed earlier by Guy as he escaped to rescue Eightball from experimenters.

"It's pretty quiet here," Eerey said. "Where are all the doctors and scientists?"

"Probably in hiding," Godwin replied. "After all, the invasion of the Ottermen is likely in full swing."

Godwin stopped at a doorway and twisted the knob. The door swung open to the sound of mayhem. Kanutian soldiers rushed strategically about the city as the Ottermen pressed their attack.

Slamming the door shut again, Godwin pressed his back against it. His pale-green face turned paler and slightly bluer. "That is not a good thing."

"What?" Eerey asked.

"Did you see that Otterman knocked out in the street?"

"I couldn't miss him. That's Shellwalker isn't it?"

Godwin stared at the ceiling and nodded. "He was supposed to retreat and make me look good. NONE of these other Ottermen knew that, or that they are working for me. Shellwalker tricked them into thinking it was a covert mission their government sent them on."

"So they'll keep attacking the city?"

Godwin nodded. "They don't know they're supposed to lose this fight."

They stood silently and listened as the sounds of battle lessened, and the sounds of victory filtered through the door. "Who won?" Godwin wondered aloud. He carefully twisted the handle and peeped out, only to be greeted by a face on the other side.

"Gah!" Godwin said in surprise.

"We won sir!" Ignatius said, his face beaming with pride. "We've routed the Ottermen!"

Godwin pulled himself together and pulled at the collar of his jacket. "Of course we won," he replied. "We are Kanutians!"

The prince strode into the street, strewn with injured Kanutian soldiers and Ottermen. Eerey followed.

Godwin looked at Ignatius. "Call the meeting, General," Godwin ordered. "I have some sad news to relay to the people of Kanutia."

"I'm not a General, sir," Ignatius humbly reminded.

"You are now. Well done, son!" Ignatius looked up at Godwin's incongruous statement. The prince could not be the soldier's father. Ignatius was twice Godwin's age.

"Call the meeting, General," Ignatius ordered. "I have some sad news to relay to the people of Kanutia."

Fifteen minutes later, Godwin stood on the top stair above the town square. A sizable crowd of Kanutians milled about below.

Godwin raised his hands dramatically above his head and began to speak. "Kanutians, we have won the day against the invaders. Our city is safe again-for the nonce. The soldiers of our fair island showed courage and heroism in battle that is unparalleled in the history of Kanutia."

A roar of approval erupted from the crowd. Godwin allowed this to die out before speaking again. "On this wondrous day, I am disheartened to bring forth a tragedy to you. The citizens of Kanute Island will certainly mourn deeply, as will I, the passing of my dear sister."

This sentence brought a collective gasp. Sobbing soon followed Godwin wiped away a tear Eerey felt certain never appeared. "Be strong Kanutians. The late Queen Maurine would beg this of you. The sad event comes at a difficult time for our community. Left without a leader, the next attack of the Ottermen will prove devastating.

"Being trained for military affairs, I am best suited to lead the defense of the island. This leaves the throne empty while I lead the battle. I humbly introduce to you the young girl, Eridona S. Tocsin, to act as Queen through this crisis."

"What makes her qualified?" An unidentified female voice rang from the crowd. "I could do that job!"

Godwin nodded. "Indeed you could, unidentified female voice. As next in natural progression to the throne, I am taking Maurine's place. That makes me King Godwin, and I choose Eridona…"

"Eerey," Eerey interjected.

"…Eerey Tocsin as queen as she is my betrothed."

"We're not betrothed!" Eerey whispered severely. "I never agreed to that!"

"Let us speak of this at an appropriate time my dear," Godwin said lowly. He turned to address the crowd again. "We will have a day of mourning for my dearly departed sister…"

"We can't have a whole day of morning!" another unidentified voice replied. "A morning's only part of a day!"

Godwin held a hand up to silence the speaker. "A day of m-o-u-r-n-i-n-g Sir!" We have much planning for the protection of the city. Return to your homes, and be watchful for danger. The city is now under a curfew!"

Godwin gestured to General Ignatius to gather his troops and clear the street before grabbing Eerey by the arm and leading her into the throne room.

Shutting the door behind them, he turned to her. "Do not forget I am in charge, and our agreement that your friends and family would be safe only stands in relation to the degree of your cooperation. I will appreciate no further outbursts from you," he grinned, "and so too will your loved ones."

Biting her tongue and her lip, Eerey nodded. "What am I to do now, oh King Godwin?"

He pointed to the ornate squid chair. "You are to sit there and adjudicate problems in the civil government."

"This new government doesn't strike me as very civil," Eerey reminded. "Martial law rarely is."

Godwin waved the sentence away with his hand. "It is not martial law. If you do your job as queen correctly, it need not come to that. Good day." Godwin haughtily strode out the door, joined just outside by a pair of soldier escorts for his protection.

Chapter XXII
BOILING POINT OF SALTWATER

As the door slammed shut another door in the room opened, allowing a young Kanutian woman of about twenty years to enter. She bowed to Eerey as the latter moved to the throne. "I am here to assist your highness. Your wish is my command."

Eerey sat in the golden throne shaped like a giant squid. Eerey looked at the bowing woman. "If my wish is your command, I wish to never see you bow to me again. It is very unbecoming."

The woman stood erect with some apprehension. "As you wish, your highness."

Eerey smiled. "What are you-a genie? If I get three wishes, I wish you'd forget about calling me 'your highness'. You're actually taller than me at any rate."

The woman looked sheepish. "What may I call you, oh Queen?"

"Queen is fine," Eerey decided. "You may call me by my name. It's Eerey."

"Eerie?"

"That's right. Although I must admit I'm not good at acting superior. I'd rather we were friends. To be friends, I need to know your name."

"My name is Ilsa," Ilsa replied, "and I'd like very much to be friends."

Eerey descended from her throne. She walked over to Ilsa and offered her hand. "It's nice to meet you, Ilsa."

Ilsa accepted Eerey's hand. "It's nice to meet you too."

Eerey retired again to the throne. "Tell me about yourself, Ilsa."

Ilsa tilted her head. "There's not much to tell, really. I grew up here in the city and haven't been farther than the reed forest." She paused for a long moment before continuing. "Wouldn't you rather hear what I know about you?"

Eerey stood her to feet. "What!? How would you know about me?"

Shrug. "Well, not you in particular, but your family's lineage."

Eerey's eyes narrowed. She sat down again. "How would you know about my family?"

"My last name is Tocsin."

Eerey gasped. "I have never heard of another family with the Tocsin surname. How is that possible?"

"It is entirely possible because we are related of course," Ilsa said. "I have done much study into family lineage. It interests me."

Eerey waved the notion away with her hand. "That's too much of a coincidence."

"It would be an amazing coincidence," Ilsa agreed. "Remember that your being here is no coincidence. You were brought here by Godwin. He explained everything to me."

"Yes, but only after leaving the Cryptoid Zoo. I wasn't brought there."

It was Ilsa's turn to gasp in surprise. "You weren't?"

Eerey sat down again. "Do you think I was brought to the zoo?"

"I don't know," Ilsa admitted. "All I do know is that you were brought to the island on purpose. It wouldn't surprise me if you were brought to the zoo on purpose."

"How could I have been brought to the zoo on purpose?" Eerey asked. "Why would I have been brought there? That all seemed to be an unfortunate coincidence."

"Maybe it was a purposeful coincidence," Ilsa suggested. "Like fate or something."

"I don't believe in fate."

"It's not as if you have a choice."

"I always have a choice. We all do."

Ilsa shrugged. "If you choose to say so. You don't seem happy to be here."

"I'm happy to be anywhere," Eerey replied.

"You chose to be queen," Ilsa said, "but you don't seem happy about it."

"Not if I'm forced to do it," Eerey admitted. "I chose to because my friends and cousin were in danger." Eerey looked past Ilsa. "Well, not all of my friends are in danger after all! Hello Guy."

"Hi Eerey," the invisible boy replied.

The disembodied voice startled Ilsa and she retreated backwards until meeting the wall. "What's that!?"

Eerey smiled. "It's okay, Ilsa! Meet my friend Guy. He's an invisible boy only I can see."

Guy smiled, but Ilsa couldn't see it. "Pleased to meet you, Ilsa."

Ilsa moved away from the wall. Her eyes searched for Guy. "Hello," she said. "I'm pleased to meet you too."

"What are you doing here, Guy?" Eerey asked. "I thought you went on the Kraken with the others."

Guy shook his head. "I snuck off when they were dropping you and Godwin here."

"Didn't Pen hypnotize you?"

"He couldn't see me sneak away before he started," Guy said. "He's not the brightest guy I know. I came back to help you escape."

"Help me escape?" Eerey said. "How do you know I want to leave?"

"Of course you want to leave," Guy said. "We need to help the others."

"That's why I'm here. If Godwin found out I was gone, he might harm them. I can't risk that."

"Do you think it'll help if you stay here?" Guy asked.

Eerey bit her bottom lip. "Maybe. I can't risk leaving until I have a plan to rescue the others." She tilted her head back. "I wish there were two of me. One could stay here and I could go figure it out."

Ilsa cleared her throat. "Maybe I can help." Eerey and Guy watched in amazement as Ilsa became a little shorter. Her pale green skin became a bit more olive-colored. Her dark hair brightened and became a little redder, curlier, and longer. Her face twisted and changed until she looked like Eerey, or at least a little.

"You're a doppelganger!" Eerey exclaimed.

Ilsa shook her Eerey-like head. "Just partially. I can only do small shifts in human form to look like other people. My mother's name was Cryptic, and she was a partial doppelganger like me."

"Like Mister Cryptic?" Eerey asked. "He's not a doppelganger."

"I don't know who you're talking about, but my grandfather's name was Cryptic. He was a full doppelganger and could take any form. He said that he became an earthworm once and split into six other doppelgangers. He kept his memories, but the other five forgot theirs over time and he lost track of them. Splitting is a dangerous trick for a doppelganger-there's no way to know how it will turn out."

Eerey nodded. "Just like how Pen became a starfish and split into four others."

"I don't know any Pen either," Ilsa said. "Is he another doppelganger?"

Guy said, "Hey! Maybe Pen is one of the doppelganger's your grandfather split into!"

Ilsa's eyes widened. "You mean this Pen guy might be my grandfather?"

"He could be," Eerey said. "At least partially. When Pen split, at least one of them turned out nice. His name was Pon. We could try to find out if we see him again."

Ilsa clapped. "That'd be great! Do you promise?"

"I promise to try to find out what I can, if you'll promise to let me take over again when I come back."

Guy gasped. "You want to come back, Eerey?"

Eerey shrugged. "Maybe. I just don't want to miss any chances before I decide."

"Decide!?" Guy stamped his foot. "What's to decide? If Maurine comes back, she'll be queen!"

"As you said; 'if'." Eerey pushed her glasses up.

"You don't really want to end up with Godwin, do you?" Guy asked.

"Who says I want to end up with anyone?" Guy looked at the floor as Eerey said this. Her eyes softened. "I mean, really. I'm young yet, and I enjoy my own company fine. I can worry about ending up with someone later, though I'd probably want to start something rather than ending with anything."

"Well," Guy said, "I wanted to tell you something."

With her invisible friend in tow, Eerey twisted the handle to the outside. "It will have to wait, Guy. Let's get out of here first."

They walked out onto the stairs and began to descend as the street, filled again with the noises of battle.

"What's that?" Eerey wondered aloud as she tried to peer in the direction of the sound. "Are the Ottermen attacking the city again?"

A group of a dozen Kanutians rushed past the stairs. Eerey pulled her hand free from Guy's and became visible.

Guy tried to grasp her hand again, but she waved his away. "What are you doing?" he asked.

"I'm doing what I said I would. Just because Godwin forced me into being queen doesn't relieve me of my duties to the Kanutian people."

The group continued to rush past them on the stairs. "Halt!" she ordered. "Report to me what is happening."

The group halted and looked up at their queen. One of the women curtsied as the others bowed. "Oh, Queen Eridona," she said, "young Krakens are attacking the city! Godwin and his forces are attempting to fight them off!"

"Go!" Eerey ordered. "Find a place to hide! Let the soldiers battle the Krakens, but be ready to fight if they lose!"

A soldier rushed past before halting at the sight of Eerey. He bowed his head. "We are under attack, my Queen!"

"Yes, I know. Give me your spear gun."

Guy's eyes widened as the soldier met Eerey and handed over his weapon. "Why are you doing this, Eerey?"

Looking over the weapon, Eerey replied, "For the Kanutians." With that, she rushed down to street to see what was going on for herself.

The Kanutian soldiers battled the young Krakens to the best of their ability. These were not like those Eerey and her friends encountered earlier. These were gray in color, while young krakens were red. They were about half the size of the ones that chased them. Godwin stood at the front line, with General Ignatius struggling against the crustaceans. Eerey watched Godwin closely. "They're not trying to attack him," she whispered to Guy as he rushed to her side.

"What does that mean?" Guy asked.

"It means we need to find the Aunt Alice." Eerey turned and rushed away from the battle.

Chapter XXIII
LOBSTER TALK

Guy followed Eerey as she rushed away. "Why do we need the Aunt Alice? How are we going to get it anyway? Godwin left it damaged and set it afloat."

Eerey shook her head. "Godwin would never throws away anything he might find valuable. I think I know where he put it."

"Where's that?"

"The shore of young krakens."

"Where you almost got drowned?"

"Yes. You know the way better than I, Guy."

"Why would we go there? We could stay here and fight young krakens!"

"I don't want to fight them," Eerey replied. "I want to find their mother."

***

Guy and Eerey took the long journey downward through the dark, dank cave to the underground lake where the young krakens lived. They stepped onto the shore to see the young krakens gathered a ways down the shore and Aunt Alice resting on the opposite shore.

"Take my hand, Guy," Eerey said. "Let's go invisible."

Guy took her hand. "I will, but I don't know what good it will do. They can find me if I'm invisible anyway."

"Well," Eerey said, "that's for the giant Kraken. It's a machine with detection equipment. We don't know that a living Kraken can find you, as we've never tried before. If we don't make much noise, we might be fine."

To test it out, Eerey and Guy began to walk toward the Aunt Alice. The krakens gave no notice to their movements. "It's working!" Eerey whispered. "We can't swim, because that would attract their attention with the splashing."

"I wonder if the others are still aboard?" Guy mused as they approached the submarine.

"It looks like it," Eerey said. "See how there's a piece of sloughed kraken shell pushed against the hole made by the mechanical Kraken? Someone must have done that to keep the young krakens out."

"I hope everyone's alright," Guy replied. "Why would Godwin leave them alone on the ship?"

"It really wouldn't matter to him. They can't go anywhere like they are, and it's too dangerous to leave with the krakens wandering about."

"They're smart enough to figure a way out."

"Yes they are. Godwin's got a fairly large ego, and thinks everyone else isn't as smart as him. That might be his mistake."

They reached the hole and crawled under the piece of kraken shell. A spear struck the piece of shell from inside the submarine, narrowly missing Guy's head.

"Hey!" Guy objected. "Stop shooting!"

Eerey pulled free from Guy's hand and became visible. "Maybe if they can see who we are!"

"Eerey!" Edict exclaimed as he rushed at them. "I'm so glad to see you, cuz!" He hugged her tightly.

Eerey pushed him away. "Ugh! I'm glad to see you too, Edict. I'm not so glad to smell you!"

Loofah smiled as he stepped forward with the spear gun. "Told you, Edict! Good to see you too, Eerey! Sorry about the spear, Guy."

"Forget that," Eerey replied.

Guy nodded. "It's just good to see you guys again."

"We need to get this ship going again," Eerey said. She looked at the gorilla in the captain's uniform. "Can you attach that kraken shell to the ship?"

The gorilla captain grunted to one of the sailor gorillas. The latter disappeared behind a door and reappeared with what looked like a welder. He went over to the hole as the third gorilla joined him. They worked together as they started welding the kraken shell to the outside of the ship.

Edict told Eerey and Guy what happened while they were away. Godwin re-attached the Kraken's claw so the hole wouldn't leak. He carried the submarine to the underground shore. He left them here, and they put the shell up to ward off all krakens, just as Eerey suggested.

Once the gorillas finished welding the shell onto the ship, Eerey examined it. "Good. It's probably as sturdy for underwater diving as the Aunt Alice's hull."

"Not so good," Loofah replied. "Even if the shell is attached and holds, what about getting it into the water?"

Eerey waved her hand. "Oh, that's no problem. Just let me deal with it." She put her laptop-hooked-to-the-typewriter-device on a rolling table and rolled it to the control room. After a short trip outside, she recovered a discarded kraken claw, light because of its emptiness. "Lobsters shed their shells from time-to-time," she explained to Guy, who went with her. Inside the claw, she attached some electric equipment and a small steam engine to it. She talked with the gorilla captain, and in a short time had the discarded kraken claw welded to the outside of the ship. Luckily, the young krakens took no notice as the two sailor gorillas worked on the project.

"Perfect!" Eerey clapped her hands. She turned on her laptop.

Loofah walked to her side. "What are you doing? All you've got now is a sign for a seafood restaurant!"

"No," Eerey said. "Now, I've got a World War Two code breaking device attached to a laptop computer and a vague understanding of the language of the Krakens!"

To illustrate, she typed into the typewriter-machine wired to the laptop. The screen on the laptop responded with a list of what looked like Morse code dots and dashes. Outside the steam powered kraken claw began clicking together in rhythm.

Outside, the young krakens responded immediately, parading around in a straight line and apparently dancing.

Loofah rolled his eyes. "Great. You've got a lobster prom going."

"Just give me time to figure out the language," Eerey replied. She typed into the machine again, and the krakens moved toward the Aunt Alice.

Eerey crossed her arms. "See?" The krakens arrived at the submarine and began hitting it with their claws.

Loofah laughed. "See what?"

Eerey frowned and started typing into the machine again. "I must not have the dialect right! They'll tear the ship apart!"

"Well, tell them to stop it!" Edict said.

"I'm trying! I didn't have time to learn more than a few words from our last encounter with the young krakens!"

"Are you sure it's a language?" Guy asked.

"Sure?" Eerey asked. "No. It sure felt like one, though! Let's hope it is, and that I can decipher it!"

"What if it isn't?" Loofah asked. "What if you don't decipher it in time?"

Her fingers worked furiously as hair fell into Eerey's eyes. "If it isn't, or if I don't decipher it in time, then we'll be eaten alive by the young krakens!"

The krakens continued to beat the side of the stranded submarine. Eerey continued to beat the keys of the antique code breaking machine. The recycled claw snapped open and shut in concert with Eerey's typing. The steam engine causing it to open and shut spit steam into the air. It clapped out a succession of sounds before falling silent. The krakens likewise stopped striking the ship.

"Why did it stop?" Edict asked.

"I'm done," Eerey said. "That message should be the right one."

The gigantic lobsters formed a line next to the ship and began pushing it with their claws. It inched toward the water until it slipped in. The gorilla captain huffed furiously at the pair of sailor gorillas. They rushed off to the engine room and the gorilla captain took the helm.

In moments, the motors rumbled to life. The submarine moved forward under the gorilla's guidance. Peering out the side ports, the group saw the krakens standing on the shore. They clicked their claws open and shut in the air above them.

"They're waving goodbye!" Loofah said.

"That's ridiculous!" Eerey replied. "They're not intelligent enough to know what it means." Despite her words, she waved out the windows with Loofah and Edict. The Aunt Alice slipped beneath the surface of the water.

ChapterXXIV
RHYME OF THE ANCIENT MARINE LIGHTHOUSE

Edict sighed. "Okay. We're underway. Where are we going today?"

"Your poem rhymes Edict," Eerey said, "but it's no Yeats. We are going to the birthplace of krakens."

"Aren't they born here?" Loofah asked.

"I don't see their parents," Eerey replied. "They might be born here, but I know where their mother lives."

Edict plopped into a convenient chair. "How do you know?"

Eerey found a chair as well, and put on her seatbelt. "I saw her eyes."

Loofah snorted. "Where? In the fridge?"

Eerey sighed. "No, but that's really funny. You guys couldn't see them, but I saw them when we followed the Kraken into the whirlpool. The light came from her eyes. They were like gigantic rubies."

Eating a Chasville Gnaw candy bar he found in storage, Guy walked into the room. He threw a bar to Edict. Edict caught it as it suddenly appeared in the air. "Whoa!" Edict said in surprise. "Thanks Guy!

"You're welcome," Guy said. "I know you like them. What are you talking about?"

Loofah chuckled. "Eerey says she saw the giant eyes of a giant lobster!"

"They glowed!" Eerey objected. "Those were the lights in the whirlpools. She was the mother of the krakens, I'm sure of it!"

A piece of chocolate fell off Edict's lip when he shrugged. "Might be true, Loofah."

"It couldn't be!" the orangutaur returned. "The lobster would have to be enormous!"

"Maybe a mile or two long," Eerey said.

Loofah guffawed. "A mile long or more? That's ridiculous! I meant the size of a fire hydrant or so!"

Edict took another bite of sugary goodness. "Doesn't matter if it's ridiculous or not if it's true. Duck-billed platypuses are ridiculous too, but they're real."

Loofah snorted. "You two are ridiculous. I'll believe it if you give me a Chasville Gnaw."

Rummaging through his pockets, Guy produced one of the bars and threw it to Loofah. "Now do you believe?" Guy asked.

"Sure," Loofah said as he unwrapped the candy and took a bite. "Whatever you say."

"It's not polite to talk with your mouth full," Eerey reminded.

"It's not polite to make things up," Loofah said.

Eerey pointed toward the pair of lights in the distance. "We'll know soon enough whether I made it up or not. Then you'll have to eat something less pleasant than candy. You'll have to eat your words."

The orangutaur shoved the rest of the bar in his mouth and chewed in silence for long moments. As they approached, they felt again the tug of the whirlpool on the submarine. The gorilla wearing the captain's hat strained against the current as he tried to keep the submarine from tipping over.

As they entered the opening of the whirlpool, Eerey peered into the shining lights. "See," she said, "I told you."

Loofah looked into the spots of light as he held onto a chair bolted to the floor. "See what? All I see are a couple of lights."

Eerey nodded. "I forgot. You guys can't see as well in the dark as I can. You'll see them soon, though."

Soon, the 'soon' Eerey predicted arrived. The Aunt Alice moved away from the whirlpools and into the darkness. With the front lantern on the ship they could see the massive nose of the lobster. "There's its nose," Eerey said. Now that the Aunt Alice moved away from the swirling water, they could see that the whirlpools came out of a pair of massive, nostril-like holes directly below the glowing, red eyes.

"Yeah," Loofah agreed. "How do we know it's attached to a mile-long lobster, though?"

Edict tilted his head and squinted. "It looks like it is for one thing. It's pretty dark out there, though. Might just be the head."

"If it is a mile-long lobster," Loofah said, "and I still don't know if it is, why hasn't anyone seen one before?"

"Maybe a bunch of people have and not survived," Eerey suggested. "There are stories from Norway about ships mistakenly landing on them. They figured it wasn't an island when the whole island sunk beneath their feet.

"This kraken might just be hiding in this deep cave. Not many people get down this far you know, and it's not safe for krakens to float around like unsettled real-estate. Besides, the ocean covers most of the planet. To find this cave and this kraken would be worse than find a needle in a haystack if it didn't move much."

Loofah huffed. "Still, just because you see a head doesn't mean there's a body."

"That's true," Edict said. "Still, it's a place to start anyway."

Loofah peered into the gloom. "I don't see a claw anywhere. A kraken that big has a large claw, I'll bet."

Eerey shuddered. "Don't say that!"

The ship shuddered as a gigantic claw grasped the ship in its tip with a quick motion. "I told you not to say that," Eerey reminded.

Loofah slid across the floor on his horseshoes. "You should have told me that before I said it!"

Eerey struck the keys of the antique typing machine and the laptop's screen displayed letters. The claw attached to the submarine clacked a message. After a moment, another enormous claw appeared in front of the ship. It clacked together, sending an intense, painfully loud vibration through the ship.

Eerey furiously typed into the machine again.

"That was too loud!" Edict shouted.

"I know!" Eerey replied. "I asked if she could clack quieter!"

The enormous claw clacked again, softer than before. This time the vibration merely buzzed loudly, as if a bee flew into their ears or Guy stood under a streetlight.

Eerey pushed down a key and a nonsensical series of figures and numbers appeared on the screen. "Great," she said. "The kraken only speaks Norwegian."

"Don't you know Norwegian, Eerey?" Edict asked.

"No. I know Portuegese. It's pretty different." Eerey shrugged. "That's okay though. I'll use a translating program."

Eerey struck a series of antique keys and the laptop screen responded with words on the screen. It changed the characters into four words, but not in English.

"I can't read that," Loofah chimed in. "It doesn't make sense!"

"I think she's asking us who we are, what we want, and why she should help us." Eerey explained. "She said 'I you not know'."

"You got all that from four short words?" Loofah snorted. "You couldn't me understand if I said that."

Edict pushed at Loofah's shoulder. "You don't have to talk. You can shut up if you want to."

"Why don't you do that?" Loofah asked.

Eerey pushed her hair back. "I don't care what you two do. If you're going to distract me I do care if you do it here. If you're going to be distracting, there are other rooms to be distracting in. If you want to stay here, then please be quiet."

"Sorry Eerey," Edict said. "We'll shut up."

Loofah opened his mouth to say something. Edict put his hand over Loofah's mouth.

"Thank you. The laptop is in translation mode so I can send in Norwegian and receive messages in Portuguese. I'll tell you two what it says in English." Eerey began typing again. The claw attached to the ship clacked out a code. "I told her my name is Alice, as it represents the submarine. If she finds out it's a ship, it could be bad. She might know what humans are. She might not like them."

The great claw of the kraken clacked out a reply. It appeared on the screen in Norwegian.

"What'd she say?" Edict asked.

"She said 'hello'."

Loofah peered at the computer screen. "Hey! That's not Norwegian at all! It's just English, but it's upside down and backwards!"

Eerey shrugged as she typed. "I just wanted to see if you'd figure it out. You did, and I'll give you a kewpie doll next chance I get."

"No need to get sarcastic," the orangutaur replied.

Eerey finished typing and turned around. "No need, but I enjoy it. Can't you and Edict go find some seaweed to play with? I'm trying to have a discussion here and you keep distracting me."

"Leave her alone you two," Guy interjected.

With a start, Edict turned to the invisible boy. "I forgot you were here, Guy. It makes it difficult when you don't say anything."

"I've been thinking," Guy replied, "and I've kept quiet so Eerey can work."

Eerey nodded. "Thank you, Guy. I don't mean to be rude to you Loofah or to you either Edict. It is important that I don't anger the mile-long crustacean with glowing eyes that's holding us in its claw."

Edict nodded. "You're probably right." He nudged Loofah. "We should go to the game room."

"I don't think it's a mile-long anyway," Loofah grumbled as they walked out of the room. "It's probably just made of rubber cement and balsa wood."

Edict turned. "Who would do that?"

Orangutaur shrug. "Somebody with too much time on their hands, plus a lot of rubber cement and a forest of balsa wood, might have been bored." Edict laughed as he shut the door behind them.

Eerey sighed and looked at Guy. "Now I can work in peace."

"I think you hurt their feelings," the invisible boy replied as the gorilla captain brushed past him.

"I hope there will be time to make it up for it later. The conversation is not going well with the kraken."

"What did she say?"

"She said she ate a glowing rock that fell from the sky when she was young. Apparently, it tasted good. It sounds radio-active, and that could be why she's so large. There used to be a city that used her for a lighthouse and fed her, but the city and its people sank. She doesn't remember when. When she got too old to hunt for food, she found this massive cave down here. She kept growing and growing, and now she can't walk anymore. She can't swim anymore. All she can do is think and lay eggs. She mainly eats plankton for food now. That, and the occasional fish she captures or whatever is attracted by the light in her eyes. She thinks we're a fish."

"But we're not," Guy pointed out.

"I know that, but she's not convinced yet."

Guy looked out of a side port window. "Uh, Eerey...I think we have bigger problems..."

"That doesn't seem possible. This kraken's pretty big." Eerey looked at her invisible friend and through the window Guy stared out. The nuclear kraken floated outside the ship. Dozens of grey krakens floated around it.

The nuclear kraken clacked its claws together. The coding machine tapped out an interpretation on its keys. The message appeared on the screen. Eerey read it with her eyes. "It's Godwin, and he's not talking to us. He's talking to the giant kraken. He says 'hello mother'."

Chapter XXV

INVISIBLE WATER

Eerey typed furiously on the code machine as a voice came out of the air. "Hello Eerey."

Eerey stopped typing and looked around. "Godwin!"

"I bet you are surprised that I can speak to the Kraken. Perhaps that is just your ego, just as you are surprised I thought to put a speaker and microphone in the Aunt Alice. I thought you would come back to that rust-bucket."

Eerey returned to typing in the machine. She spoke into the air as she did so. "It's not as cool a trick as you're making it out to be, Godwin. To place a bug on the ship is not very hard. The only surprise is I didn't think about it. How long did it take you to figure out kraken language anyway?"

"Nevermind that," Godwin retorted. "I do not want to destroy you, but if you will not cooperate, you leave me no choice."

"You're always left a choice, whether or not I leave you one," Eerey reminded. "You tried to leave me no choice, but you failed. I made my choice."

"You chose to risk yourself and your friends."

"I'd rather risk myself and my friends than allow you to make the choices for us."

"Why?" Godwin asked. "I am a pretty good guy if you get to know me." He sighed. "I wish we could be friends. Now I have to destroy the Aunt Alice."

The gorilla captain looked at Eerey as she replied, "If you think you can."

"I did it before. Do you think I can't do it again?"

Eerey shrugged. "Anybody can get lucky once."

"Lucky!? I will show you it is not luck at all! Then you will be sorry!"

"You can use contractions, you know. It'll make your speeches faster-and less boring."

"A real gentleman never uses contractions, and I'll show you boring!"

With that, the nuclear kraken moved toward the Aunt Alice. The gorilla captain twisted the wheel to bring the submarine into a battle position.

Loofah and Edict rushed in. "What's going on!?"

Eerey typed into the machine. The discarded claw clacked a message to the mother kraken. "We're under attack by Godwin in the nuclear kraken along with the smaller robot krakens he built."

"I wasn't asking about that," Edict replied, "but that makes things even worse!"

Loofah nodded his head. "Yeah. I was talking about the giant shark and the Ottermen!"

Eerey looked out one of the viewing ports alongside the submarine. "What is going on?"

"I have no idea," Godwin said through the speaker. "It doesn't look good for you."

"You're starting to use contractions," Eerey said. "Maybe you're getting nervous?"

Godwin laughed over the speaker. "Why would I be nervous? These are my allies!"

The mother kraken's claw separated and the Aunt Alice slid free.

"What!?" Godwin exclaimed. "She wasn't supposed to let go!"

"I guess," Loofah said, "that your allies are changing sides."

"Yes," Eerey agreed. "I guess you weren't listening to the conversation between the kraken and I while you were distracted talking with me."

"It doesn't matter!" Godwin shouted. "You and your friends are doomed!" The nuclear kraken moved toward the Aunt Alice as the gorilla captain spun the wheel to bring the helm to point its swordfish-like snout at it.

The robot krakens followed the nuclear kraken. The gorilla captain pushed a lever forward all the way. The submarine lurched and headed at the nuclear kraken.

The move took everyone in the submarine off guard and most off their feet. Only Loofah remained standing. He slid on the metal surface, his horseshoes making an awful screeching sound against the floor and kicking up sparks.

He slammed into the wall and looked at his hooves. "These are new shoes! Now I'll have to replace them!"

"Don't worry about it, pal," Edict said. "Worry about it when we're out of this mess!"

Loofah fell down with everyone else as the Aunt Alice struck the nuclear kraken in the belly. The long metal snout skewered the kraken machine, exposing the electric parts beneath the shell. Water rushed in as the mother kraken clacked her massive claw furiously and loudly.

"What's she saying?" Guy shouted as he stood.

Eerey pulled herself up to the metal counter; glad she secured the laptop and code machine to it. The code machine clicked away and translated the claw's clacking. "She's angry," Eerey replied. "She can see now what I told her was true. Godwin tricked her into thinking it...he was her son. She doesn't like being tricked."

"So what?" Loofah said. "Look at my shoes!"

"It's all over, Eerey." Godwin said. The nuclear kraken's claw twisted. It grabbed onto the submarine and began drilling.

The Ottermen fired their weapons at the nuclear kraken. The claw let go of the Aunt Alice and the submarine backed away as the gorilla captain pulled the lever back.

Eerey smiled. "It looks as if your friends aren't on your side, Godwin."

"It doesn't matter," Godwin sneered. "They can't take on the nuclear kraken and win!"

A dozen robot krakens swam toward the attacking Ottermen. The dazzling display of laser fire striking at the mechanical crustaceans brightened the vast cavern. Those metal krakens they missed grasped at the Ottermen with their claws and pulled them to the cavern bottom.

"You will not get away with this brother," a voice came over the radio.

"Maurine?" Godwin asked, curiosity filling his voice.

The giant shark smiled as it swam next to the nuclear kraken. Maurine sat on Rover's back as the shark's gold tooth gleamed brightly. Maurine wore a glass helmet and her beautiful gown streamed delicately in the water. "Yes, Godwin. It was no great feat to escape that sunken derelict ocean liner where you left me."

"You were hypnotized!" Godwin replied.

Maurine shrugged. "Hypnotism wears off, you know. Besides, it was mesmerism. It is not as strong."

Inside the nuclear kraken Godwin looked toward Pen. The doppelganger shrugged his reply. The prince gritted his teeth.

"It does not matter. My kraken-bots will triumph. Failing that, my nuclear kraken will finish you for good!"

The kraken bots surrounded the Aunt Alice and began pulling at the metal panels. "They'll pull us apart!" Edict said.

"What'll we do then?" Loofah asked.

Eerey bit her lip until it turned pale. "We won't do anything then. Then it will be all over for us."

"I won't allow that," Guy said invisibly. Eerey watched him kneel on the floor and touch its metal surface. The ship began to shimmer and become translucent as a buzzing tone filled the air and grew louder.

Eerey watched Guy as his face scrunched in painful concentration. "Guy! Don't do that! You don't know what it will do to you!"

Guy smiled wryly. "I can guess. It might kill me, but I won't allow Godwin to kill my friends." A tear glimmered in the corner of his eye as he looked at Eerey. "I won't let you die."

"Guy!" Loofah said to where Eerey gazed. The orangutaur had to shout over the buzzing as it grew louder and louder. "It won't matter if the ship's invisible! The robot krakens can still find us! They are sensitive!"

"I'm not trying to hide from them!" Guy replied. "I'm trying to use their senses against them!"

Instinctively, the Ottermen and the giant shark with Maurine on its back swam through the whirlpools to escape. The robots, having no instincts of their own, stayed to tear at the Aunt Alice.

The buzzing grew too loud for talking. Everyone had to hold their ears as they turned invisible. The ship's walls disappeared altogether. The robot krakens appeared at the sides. They stopped working and began to fall off the invisible submarine as they started to become invisible themselves. Eerey watched as even Guy disappeared before her eyes. Even she could not see him anymore.

"Guy!" she shouted. The buzzing drowned out her shout. Eerey rushed to where she last saw Guy. The sound made her ears hurt and she lost her balance. She fell to the floor against something invisible.

"Watch it!" Loofah yelled over the buzzing. "I'm right here!"

"I can't see you!" Eerey shouted.

"Join the club!"

The feeling was strange as Eerey held her ears. It looked as if she floated in the center an air bubble in the water but couldn't touch the sides. Guy turned the water immediately around the submarine invisible as well. The buzzing grew in volume, but Eerey felt sick and couldn't stand. "We've got to stop him, Loofah!"

"I know," the orangutaur replied. "but I can't! I think I might throw up! That buzzing is making me dizzy!"

Eerey felt herself unable to move. She watched as the nuclear kraken sparked electricity before going dark. It sank toward the seafloor, but the long reach of the mother kraken grasped the machine.

The buzzing slowly abated and soon became tolerable. First, the water became visible again. Then the sides of the ship returned. Finally, everyone and everything on the ship with the exception of Guy came into view. They stood unsteadily to their feet.

"Guy!" Eerey said too loudly as her ears were still ringing. She began walking over the floor. "Say something! I can't see you!"

"I can look for him cuz," Edict offered. He started crawling on the floor, sniffing around like a bloodhound.

"You look silly," Loofah said.

Edict looked up and snorted. "I don't care. Guy's my friend, and he may be hurt! I'll look as stupid as I can if it means it'll help him!"

Loofah shrugged before bending his legs and crawling on the floor with Edict, sniffing for Guy. After long moments of this, Edict looked up. "I didn't find a thing. I think he's gone, Eerey."

A tear gathered in the corner of Eerey's eye. "How could he be!?" she said. "He could only turn invisible!"

Edict and Loofah turned their heads and shrugged unhappily. "He must have went past invisible," Edict said, "and gone to intangible."

Chapter XXVII
SURFACING LEVIATHAN

A loud, crackling sound interrupted the conversation as a plume of dirty water blackened the windows. The code machine clattered out a message. Walking to the laptop screen, Eerey read the message aloud. "You are not kraken. You are humans in kraken clothing."

A giant shadow of the mother kraken's claw fell through the murky waters. The mother kraken grasped the Aunt Alice yet again. The ship lurched and moved upward.

"The mother kraken is swimming!" Eerey exclaimed.

"Swimming!?" Edict said. "I thought it couldn't even move!"

"Well," Loofah said, "it can."

Eerey nodded. "Yes. We're its captives for the moment. I only hope it's not for long."

The ocean cleared as the mother kraken swam out of the cave where most of the cloud of mud remained. Sunlight pierced the dark waters from far above. The nuclear kraken didn't move as it hung limply in the other gargantuan claw.

It became brighter as they neared the ocean's surface glittering in the sun. They could see the mother kraken in her entirety. Eerey could not tell its exact size, but a pencil drawing tapped out on the antique radar machine could not even fit the entire body into a page. It might not have been an entire mile, but it was huge.

They watched through the submarine's ports as the mother kraken broke the surface of the water. The other claw still held the unmoving nuclear kraken. The mother kraken seemed still as well. It shut its eyes, turning off the lights. Very slowly, the other claw laid the nuclear kraken on its back and clicked its claw together.

Eerey went to the code machine as it began to click a single word. She read the computer screen aloud. "Dying."

Eerey typed into the machine, saying the message aloud as she did so. "We did not mean to hurt you."

The mother kraken clicked her claws together and the code machine clattered a message. Eerey read it aloud, "It is okay. Should not move."

"Can we help?" Eerey said as she typed. The enormous claw slid silently into the water. Eerey dropped her head. "She's gone."

"Should we get out?" Loofah said.

The gorillas ran into the room. Everyone looked up in surprise when the gorilla captain said in a gruff voice, "Are you kidding? She'll sink like a stone in a few minutes! Of course we shouldn't get out! We've got to be on the ship if she sinks! It's the safest place!"

"Yes! Eerey said. "Godwin's still in the nuclear kraken, though! We should help him and get away in the Aunt Alice before the mother kraken sinks."

"Good," the gorilla captain said. "We'll stay here."

"What!?" Edict said. "We might need your help!"

The gorilla captain shrugged. "A captain goes down with his ship. We'll keep the engine going while you help the others in the kraken. Just hurry and come back."

They dropped the gangplank out the side of the Aunt Alice. Eerey and Edict followed Loofah off the submarine. The gorillas followed them, but nobody asked why. Eerey rushed over to the nuclear kraken as she saw one of the claws open partway. Godwin struggled to come out of it, but it was too small a hole. He looked at Eerey as the young girl rushed over. "Eerey!"

"I think you're stuck, Godwin!" Eerey shouted. "Give me your hand!"

He thrust his hand out. "If you think it will help."

Eerey grasped his hand and pulled. "It's no use trying," she said as she kept trying. Sweat beaded on her brow. She scrunched her face and pulled with all her might.

Godwin smiled sadly. "I didn't think so." Loofah, and Edict rushed up behind Eerey. The prince held his hand up and shook his head. "Forget it fellas and gorillas. It will not do any good."

Eerey laughed as a tear fell down her cheek. "Always the gentleman. You can use contractions you know."

"I know." Godwin looked at Eerey's companions. "Can you give me a last moment alone with Eerey?"

The others moved away as Eerey knelt next to Godwin. The gorillas climbed the gangplank back into the submarine. Edict shook his head.

"I did love you, Eerey," Godwin said.

Eerey looked into Godwin's eyes. "No you didn't. You didn't even know me. You were infatuated. You loved yourself."

Godwin laughed and coughed. "You are probably right. Allow me to tell myself a little white lie as a last wish?"

Eerey nodded and smiled. "Okay."

"I know," Godwin said between short breaths, "that you did not love me. Do you think you might have eventually?"

Eerey slowly nodded. "Maybe if you didn't try to control me. I didn't love you, but I liked you at first. You can't control love, just like you can't control the ocean. I can't figure out the ocean, and I don't think I'll figure out love for many more years."

"I wonder," Godwin said, "if anyone ever does."

Eerey nodded. "I believe they do. I love my family, and that's a start."

Godwin let out a yelp as the nuclear kraken lurched. He looked again at Eerey. "Tell Maurine that I love my family too."

Eerey started to reply, but the nuclear kraken started to slide. "No!" She had to let go of Godwin's hand as Edict grabbed her around the waist. "Come on, cuz…you don't want to go down with his ship."

Eerey struggled against her hair-covered cousin, but he was too strong for her. "Let me go Edict!"

Godwin smiled and waved goodbye as the nuclear kraken slid into the depths. "Goodbye Eerey."

"NOOOO!" Eerey shrieked. She twisted out of Edict's grip and fell to her knees on the mother kraken's armored back. Edict dropped his head.

Loofah cleared his throat. "I thought you didn't like him, Eerey."

Eerey pushed herself to her feet. "I did like him. He was a bit of a snob, but I did like him. If he'd treated me nicer I might even have wanted to be his friend."

They stood looking into the water for signs of Godwin's fate. The liquid softly washed the kraken's black armor, offering no comfort.

Chapter XXVIII
THE FLOATING ISLAND SINKS

Something enormous erupted from the surface of the ocean, sending a huge wave over the kraken's back. Eerey and Edict could only grasp an edge of the black armor and hold on. Loofah dug his horseshoes into the surface and managed to remain upright, though he slid across the surface from the force washing over him.

When the water rolled off the armor, Eerey and Edict stood uneasily to their feet. The Aunt Alice washed over the side and was gone, with the talking gorillas aboard.

"I've lost my glasses!" Eerey said.

Edict nodded. "We've lost the submarine too! The gorillas are on board."

"It's still seaworthy," Eerey replied. "They'll be okay. They are good sailors, whether or not they talk."

Eerey peered toward the object. Rover rested with his nose in the water as Maurine, Pon and Ilsa stepped off the giant shark's back. Rover carried the defunct nuclear kraken in his teeth. Godwin remained stuck in the claw. A glass helmet covered his head.

Eerey saw that the prince didn't move. "Godwin!" She turned to Maurine. "Is he okay?"

The returning queen nodded. "He's just unconscious. We cannot get him out of the claw, but he seems to be fine otherwise."

Eerey nodded. "I'm glad. I thought he was a goner!"

"Not a goner," Maurine replied. "Just a brat. He is still my brother, and I love him. He'll have to make up for the damage he has done, but hopefully he will figure out a better way to do things in the future. Ilsa told me what happened. Thanks for taking over in my absence."

Eerey shrugged. "I'm ready to let you have your throne, although it was interesting to be royalty for a while. I wanted Godwin and Pen and others to think that I wanted to be queen, but I didn't. Not really. If they thought I did Godwin might give me more freedom. I needed that if I was going to save my friends. I didn't want Ilsa to know, because I wasn't sure if I could trust her. It seems that you don't have all that much freedom and a lot of responsibility."

"It has its plusses and minuses," Maurine said. "If Godwin had just asked, I might have let him have it. He has a notion that it is great, but it is not easy. Nothing worthwhile ever is."

Loofah walked over. "I see you're doing fine, Pon-if you really are Pon."

Pon smiled and laughed. "I really are." He put a hand on Ilsa's shoulder. "I'm glad to meet my granddaughter."

Ilsa smiled. "He's a great guy, and I'm happy to be related to him."

Eerey sighed. "I'm happy for you. I wish we knew what happened to Guy and my parents and Mister Cryptic."

Pon handed Eerey an oyster shell wrapped in duct tape. "Here's what happened to Pen. He turned into a shellfish when he thought they might sink, and I duct taped him. As for Pin or Pan..." Pon shrugged.

"Maybe I can help with your invisible friend," Ilsa said. "I think Guy might be related to Gyges the Lydian king somehow, He had a ring that his ancestor found. It could turn the wearer invisible."

"Plato wrote about that, didn't he?" Eerey asked.

Ilsa nodded. "Plato talked about the possibility of two rings existing. In one legend, a young child swallowed a ring like that and went invisible. I don't know if Guy is related to that child, but it's worth checking out. Maybe a trip to Lydia might help you find some answers."

"Maybe," Loofah said. "How will we get there?"

Pon looked at the sky and pointed. "First you have to get out of here, and that might be an answer."

They looked and saw the plane Eerey's parents had flown away in. At the same time, one of the mother kraken's claws began clicking. Eerey took off her waterproof backpack and pulled the laptop computer out. Annoyed to be woken up, Eightball snapped at her with his teeth, but missed.

Eerey laughed at the large spider. "Calm down, Eightball! I'll let you go back to sleep!"

Maurine looked at the spider. "Is he poisonous?"

Eerey waved the idea away with her hand. "He's tame." She turned on the computer to translate what the mother kraken said. The claw clattered out a message. The words appeared on the screen, in English, but still upside down. "She says she fell asleep. She wasn't dead, just dead tired from swimming. She says it takes a lot of energy to move her enormous weight, and...uh oh!"

"'uh oh'?" Loofah asked. "That doesn't sound good!"

Eerey shook her head. "It isn't. She said goodbye!" She looked at the airplane as it flew toward a landing. "They think it's an island! If she sinks while they're landing, it won't be good! It won't be good if we're on it either, because the force of the water coming in will be tremendous!"

Loofah laughed. "Tell her to wait!"

"I can't!" Eerey replied. "I can get her signals, but the claw is on the Aunt Alice! She doesn't know we can't swim either!"

It was too late to do much of anything, as the plane roared to a landing on the mother kraken's black armor. It struck a seam on the armor and one of the tire's exploded. Eerey turned to Maurine, Pon and Ilsa. "You should go! You need to climb on Rover and get away from here before she sinks! She could be large enough to create a tidal wave!"

Maurine nodded. "Thanks for everything. I wish we could talk more! Come visit Kanutia again if you can!"

"As long I can visit and not stay if I don't want!" Eerey replied.

Maurine smiled. "Of course." The trio rushed off and climbed aboard the giant shark as the airplane landed. Eerey, Edict, and Loofah rushed to it as a rope ladder came down from the plane. Eerey's mom, wearing a gas mask, prepared to climb down.

"Stay aboard!" Eerey shouted. "This isn't an island, and it's about to sink!"

Her mother looked puzzled, but heeded her daughter's command with a nod. She shouted to the pilot's compartment. Edict reached the ladder first and began climbing. Eerey came quickly after. Loofah ran up and grabbed the rope just as the airplane gained speed. With the dexterity of an orangutan, he flung himself inside.

Eerey rushed into the cockpit as the plane began to slow again. "What are you doing dad!? We've got to get out of here!"

Her father looked at her from behind his gas mask. "We have a flat tire! The plane's just rolling on a rim now. We probably can't take off like that!"

"Well, that figures." Thinking quickly, Eerey unzipped her backpack. Eightball grumbled at the interruption.

"Sorry Eightball, but we need a wheel. Think you can do it?"

Eightball hissed as Eerey headed for the door. She set the spider on the floor next to it. "Thanks, E.B."

The spider let out a stream of webbing and descended quickly to the ground. All eight legs spinning, he rushed to the flat tire. He wrapped his legs around the wheel.

"Okay dad!" Eerey shouted. "Try it now!"

The plane's propellers began to spin faster and move forward. Eightball, tightly holding the wheel like a prey, began spinning faster and faster. So fast there was no way to tell the difference between him and the other wheels.

Water began pouring over the shell, and the wheels spit up streams as the plane struggled against time to gain air. The plane lifted off just as the mother kraken sank beneath the surface, sending a huge plume of water into the air. The resulting spray washed against the plane's belly as the landing gear retracted- wheels, Eightball and all.

Eerey returned to the cockpit. Her dad glanced at her. "Where to now?" he asked. The gasmask muffled his voice.

Eerey sat down in the co-pilot's chair. She scrunched her eyes against the sunset's light. "Can we go to Lydia? We have to find out what's happened to Guy."

Eerey's mother sighed. "You know, Eerey, we have jobs to do back home."

"Now Verna," Eerey's father replied, "we have no idea where we are. We might as well go to Lydia-at least that's somewhere. We talked about going anyway."

Eerey's mother nodded. "Sounds good enough. Let's go."

Eerey looked at her parents. "I didn't know you had jobs." She looked at the instrument panel. "And why are you wearing gas masks?"

Her father shrugged. "We flew through a pocket of methane gas. It's one of the causes for planes disappearing in the Bermuda triangle. Probably not the only reason, though. We just haven't taken the masks off yet." He looked at Eerey. "I think it makes us look sophisticated."

Eerey shrugged. "Okay."

"By the way, where is Mister Cryptic?" Loofah asked as he walked in from the back of the plane.

"Oh," Verna said in muffled tones. "Follow me."

EPILOGUE

Eerey rose and followed with Loofah. Edict sat on a chair behind the pilot's compartment and stood to go with as they walked by.

Verna opened the door to the cargo hold and waited as they all filed in. No one spoke, but looked silently on what they saw. An ornate metal horse took up most of the room. It reminded Eerey of a knight piece in chess, though it laid upon its belly with its legs folded beside. The face had a powerful or angry expression as its head tilted toward the floor. Eerey imagined the Trojan horse may have looked like this. It looked mechanical somehow, although no wires or gears showed. A row of small windows the size of drink coasters ran down the side. Eerey leaned over to look into the dark interior. She saw someone wrapped as a mummy resting comfortably inside.

"What's this?" Eerey asked.

Verna shrugged. "We think it's a sarcophagus. Or a coffin. We can't tell much more."

"I thought a sarcophagus was a coffin," Edict said.

Verna nodded her hidden face. "That's right. It's a stone coffin. We're not sure this is made of metal or stone or of anything we know. Mister Cryptic brought it on board before we left. That's him wrapped up inside."

Edict tried to look inside, but couldn't see anything. "Why is Mister Cryptic dressed like a mummy? Is he dead?"

Verna sighed again. "It's a long story."

"It's a long trip," Loofah said. "We have time."

"That's true," Verna replied. "We don't know why he's mummified, but I'm sure it's a long story. Interestingly, we think that Lydia is the place to find out. In Plato's description about Gyges' invisible ring, the ancestor found it in a sarcophagus exactly like this. A well-preserved corpse of a giant wore it. Lydia is the place where we'll find the answers to what happened to Mister Cryptic and Guy both, or at least is a good place to start."

THE END

Experience the Beginning!

Available from your favorite bookstore !

The Tocsin Codex: Book 1
Eerey Tocsin in the Cryptoid Zoo
ISBN: 1-887560-17-3

Printed in the United States
129635LV00003BB/124/P

9 781934 935170